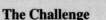

The Challenge

"Mr. Adams!"

He stopped and turned. Wild Bill Flanagan was standing there with his guns on.

"Mr. Adams," he said. "What would happen if I made you shoot with me?"

"And how would you do that, Dave?"

"By callin' you out."

"Now that wouldn't be smart, Dave," Clint said. "You're talking about doing more than just shooting at targets. Have you ever faced a man with a gun before?"

"No, I haven't," Flanagan said. "But there's always a first time. You had your first time."

"Well," Clint said, "I don't want your first time to be your last, Dave. I'm sure Julie doesn't, either."

Flanagan didn't comment, but he started to flex his hands.

"Julie's right inside the tent, Dave. You want her to watch you die?"

"I'm not talking about now, Clint," Flanagan said. "But sometime before the week is out. I think you'll shoot against me."

"Son," Clint said, "you better hope not."

DON'T MISS THESE
ALL-ACTION WESTERN SERIES
FROM THE BERKLEY PUBLISHING GROUP

THE GUNSMITH by J. R. Roberts
Clint Adams was a legend among lawmen, outlaws, and ladies. They called him . . . the Gunsmith.

LONGARM by Tabor Evans
The popular long-running series about Deputy U.S. Marshal Custis Long—his life, his loves, his fight for justice.

SLOCUM by Jake Logan
Today's longest-running action Western. John Slocum rides a deadly trail of hot blood and cold steel.

BUSHWHACKERS by B. J. Lanagan
An action-packed series by the creators of Longarm! The rousing adventures of the most brutal gang of cutthroats ever assembled—Quantrill's Raiders.

DIAMONDBACK by Guy Brewer
Dex Yancey is Diamondback, a Southern gentleman turned con man when his brother cheats him out of the family fortune. Ladies love him. Gamblers hate him. But nobody pulls one over on Dex . . .

WILDGUN by Jack Hanson
The blazing adventures of mountain man Will Barlow—from the creators of Longarm!

TEXAS TRACKER by Tom Calhoun
J.T. Law: the most relentless—and dangerous—manhunter in all Texas. Where sheriffs and posses fail, he's the best man to bring in the most vicious outlaws—for a price.

THE GUNSMITH

350

WITH DEADLY INTENT

J. R. ROBERTS

JOVE BOOKS, NEW YORK

THE BERKLEY PUBLISHING GROUP
Published by the Penguin Group
Penguin Group (USA) Inc.
375 Hudson Street, New York, New York 10014, USA
Penguin Group (Canada), 90 Eglinton Avenue East, Suite 700, Toronto, Ontario M4P 2Y3, Canada
(a division of Pearson Penguin Canada Inc.)
Penguin Books Ltd., 80 Strand, London WC2R 0RL, England
Penguin Group Ireland, 25 St. Stephen's Green, Dublin 2, Ireland (a division of Penguin Books Ltd.)
Penguin Group (Australia), 250 Camberwell Road, Camberwell, Victoria 3124, Australia
(a division of Pearson Australia Group Pty. Ltd.)
Penguin Books India Pvt. Ltd., 11 Community Centre, Panchsheel Park, New Delhi—110 017, India
Penguin Group (NZ), 67 Apollo Drive, Rosedale, North Shore 0632, New Zealand
(a division of Pearson New Zealand Ltd.)
Penguin Books (South Africa) (Pty.) Ltd., 24 Sturdee Avenue, Rosebank, Johannesburg 2196,
South Africa

Penguin Books Ltd., Registered Offices: 80 Strand, London WC2R 0RL, England

This is a work of fiction. Names, characters, places, and incidents either are the product of the author's imagination or are used fictitiously, and any resemblance to actual persons, living or dead, business establishments, events, or locales is entirely coincidental.

WITH DEADLY INTENT

A Jove Book / published by arrangement with the author

PRINTING HISTORY
Jove edition / February 2011

Copyright © 2011 by Robert J. Randisi.
Cover illustration by Sergio Giovine.

ISBN: 978-0-515-14900-5

JOVE®
Jove Books are published by The Berkley Publishing Group,
a division of Penguin Group (USA) Inc.,
375 Hudson Street, New York, New York 10014.
JOVE® is a registered trademark of Penguin Group (USA) Inc.
The "J" design is a trademark of Penguin Group (USA) Inc.

PRINTED IN THE UNITED STATES OF AMERICA

10 9 8 7 6 5 4 3 2 1

ONE

With lead whizzing around his head, Clint Adams sought cover. This was not an unusual situation for him. He figured he'd probably spent half his life dodging bullets, but that's what you get when you're known as the Gunsmith. He knew that the men he considered to be his best friends—Hickok, Earp, Masterson—had spent their lives doing the same thing. So far only Hickok had succumbed to a coward's bullet.

Clint found a big rock to hunker down behind, sat with his back to it, and listened. The shooting had stopped. He wasn't sure yet, but he had a feeling he was being shot at by two guns. To know for sure, he'd have to get them to fire again.

The one thing he was content about was that Eclipse had run far enough to be away from the action. He knew the big Darley Arabian wouldn't go too far, just far enough to be safe.

Clint had gotten out of the saddle as soon as he heard the first shot and felt the first hunk of hot lead whiz by his ear. Whoever had fired that bullet was good, had probably just

rushed the shot a bit. With somebody that good, he didn't
feel he could outrun the next shots. Better to get off the
horse and seek cover, let the horse take itself away to safety.

He didn't have his rifle. He'd made a grab for it as he
leaped from his horse, but he'd missed it. Getting old, he
told himself. He had his pistol, but he needed to be closer
for that to be of any use. Right now it was just a noise-
maker.

Who was shooting at him? That was anybody's guess.
Didn't have to be anybody he knew, and it usually wasn't.
More to the point it was usually somebody who knew
him—or who recognized him on sight, probably in the last
town he'd stopped in. That had been Jackson Bend, just
before he left New Mexico and crossed into Arizona.

Jackson Bend had been two days ago. He'd camped on
the trail since then. Why hadn't anyone tried for him before
now? Maybe while he was asleep? Instead they chose to try
to bushwhack him in broad daylight from a distance.

Obviously, the bullet that had just missed him was a
coward's bullet, as were the rest.

"You rushed it!" Cal Barnes snapped.

"I got a lot closer than you ever woulda," Harry Fields
said. "At least he's off his horse and on foot. He's ours."

"You gonna get him from here?"

"As soon as I get a clear shot."

"Why don't we move closer?"

"Because then he can use his gun," Fields said. "You
wanna face the Gunsmith when he's got his gun in his hand?"

"Not me," Barnes said.

"Well, not me, either."

Neither man wanted to get any closer to the Gunsmith
than they were right now. That was why they hadn't tried to

get to him while he camped. There was too much of a chance he'd wake up and go for that gun of his.

"We gotta get him out from behind that rock," Barnes said.

"I'll just chip away at it a little bit," Fields said, raising his rifle.

"No, don't fire," Barnes said. "You'll just waste your ammo. Besides, I don't think you can hit the rock."

"That big rock? I can, too, hit it."

"I'll bet you can't."

"How much?"

"A dollar?"

"You got a bet," Fields said.

"I'll fire first, then you," Barnes said. "First one to miss loses."

"You got a bet!"

Clint was trying to figure a way to get them to fire again when they started on their own. A bullet chipped off a piece of the boulder he was behind. Another bullet sailed by, clearly fired from a different rifle.

They alternated again, first one, then the other, which Clint found odd. It was as if they were taking turns firing at the boulder. Did they think this would spook him from his cover?

Or were they just playing some kind of game with him— or with each other?

TWO

The shooters alternated until, finally, one of them missed. The shooting stopped after that, probably to reload. Clint decided to take advantage.

He broke from cover and ran toward the hill he figured the two shooters were on.

"There!" Fields said. "You missed. You owe me a dollar."

"Yah, but I hit it almost as many times as you did," Barnes said.

"That don't matter," Fields said. "We had a bet, and you lost."

"Look!" Barnes said.

"Never mind that, you owe me a dol—"

"No, look! Adams!"

Fields turned and they both saw Clint Adams running toward them. Fields raised his rifle, aimed, and pulled the trigger. The hammer fell helplessly. Barnes raised his rifle and fired, but he was empty, too.

"Damn it!" Fields said, "Reload!"

* * *

Clint made it to the base of the hill without another shot being fired. They were most likely reloading. Neither of them had the instinct to grab their side arms. That gave him a good idea what kind of men he was dealing with.

He made his way around the hill, then started up.

"What do we do now?" Barnes asked, once they had reloaded.

"I don't see him down there," Fields said.

"He's probably on his way up here."

They stared at each other.

"Let's get to the horses!" Fields said.

"Shit, we ain't gonna get us no Gunsmith today, is we?" Barnes asked.

"We just gotta stay alive," Fields said. "We'll get 'im next time."

They ran for their horses, which they'd tied to a tree just behind them.

Clint heard the sound of horses and increased his pace up the hill. By the time he got to the top, two riders had descended the other side of the hill. They'd managed to choose correctly and avoid riding right into him.

He reached the top of the hill and watched them ride off. Two unremarkably dressed men, riding horses that were nothing special. He didn't see anything special about them that would stand out and make them easy to recognize later on.

He studied the ground around him. Their boot prints were the same, nothing unusual to make them easy to recognize. He looked further, found the tracks left by the horses. Still out of luck: no identifying marks on their hooves.

Just two men who had spotted him and decided to try and make a name for themselves by killing the Gunsmith. They were men who wouldn't mind being called bush-whackers, as long as they were known for killing him. He didn't understand that kind of thinking.

Before he left, he picked up some of their discarded shells. They looked new, but that didn't mean the weapons—probably Winchesters—had been new. He stuck a couple of them in his pocket, anyway, then started back down the hill.

When he got to the bottom, he didn't have to go looking for Eclipse. The Darley sensed the danger was gone, and had wandered back to look for him.

"How ya doin, big fella?" he asked, rubbing the horse's neck. He looked the horse over for damage and was satisfied to find none. He grabbed his canteen, took a swig, then put some in the palm of his hand for the horse.

He mounted up, and continued riding west, the direction he had originally been headed in. He could have tried to track the two bushwhackers down, but why? They'd be interchangeable with any number of men who had tried it in the past. Some of them had paid with their lives, but some had gotten away. And some of them would keep running and never try again.

What these two would do was anybody's guess, but he wasn't going to concern himself about it. He had things to do, and there were some men waiting for him in Bullhead City.

THREE

Bullhead City was small, but booming, as Clint rode in. Of course, that was no surprise. The Colorado River Festival, named after the river that ran right by the town, was taking place, and Clint had been invited because of all the activity.

Clint rode in the day before the festival was to start. He'd been told to present himself at the Bullhead Hotel and Saloon, and there'd be a room waiting for him.

He reined Eclipse in right in front of the establishment, tied him loosely to a post, and went inside with his saddlebags and rifle.

When he approached the front desk, the young clerk said, "I hope you got a reservation, sir, because we're really filled up for the festival."

"My name is Clint Adams," Clint said. "You tell me if I have a reservation."

The clerk frowned at him, but opened his book and moved his finger down his list.

"Adams, Adams . . . wait," the young man said. "*Clint* Adams?"

"That's right."

"Um, the Gunsmith?"

"Is my name there, son?"

"Oh, yes, sir," the clerk said. "You got a room waitin', all right. And I'm to have somebody take care of your horse."

"Where's the stable?" Clint asked.

"Right out back."

"Give me my key and put these saddlebags in my room," Clint said. "I'll take my horse into the stable myself."

"Yes, sir, whatever you say." He turned, plucked a key from the box on the wall. "You've got room five, sir. Overlooks the street."

"Fine," Clint said. He guessed that the town was going to be so noisy it didn't matter what room he had. And he'd noticed when he rode up that there was no outside access to the front windows.

"Tell Riff, in the stable, what your name is. He's savin' a stall for your horse."

Clint waved, went out the front door. He untied Eclipse from the post and walked him around to the stable in the back. Riff turned out to be a wizened old-timer who knew good horseflesh when he saw it.

"Yeah, I saved yuh a stall. But now that I see yer horse, I'm gonna move 'im someplace better."

"Much obliged."

"Don't thank me," Riff said. "Ain't offin I get a horse like this in my place. I gotta thank you."

Clint left Eclipse with Riff, confident that the animal was in good hands.

He walked back around to the front of the hotel and was about to go into the lobby when he decided to keep going to the saloon. A beer would go down good before he went and checked out his room.

He walked in unnoticed, because the place was jumping. That suited him. Whenever he walked into a saloon and drew attention, there was a chance some would-be gunny would notice him and decide to test him.

He approached the bar, managed to elbow himself a spot and wave to the busy bartender for a beer.

"You stayin' in the hotel?" the barman asked as he set the beer down.

"That's right."

"Name?"

"Does that matter?"

"You got a room comped?"

"Comped?"

"A complimentary room," the bartender said.

"Oh, yeah, my room's being paid for by—"

"It don't matter who," the man said. "Beer's on the house for you."

"Not going to do much business if you're giving beer away," Clint said.

"Ain't givin' it away," the man said. "It's bein' paid for, just not by you."

"Suits me."

Clint picked up the mug and washed down some trail dust. He looked out at the crowded saloon, wondering if the two would-be bushwhackers were in the crowd. He hadn't intentionally tried to track them, but their trail did lead here to Bullhead City. He didn't think he had to worry that they'd try for him in town, though. They'd do their killing from behind a tree every time.

He looked for familiar faces. This kind of activity usually brought gamblers and grifters to town, and he knew both.

He didn't see anyone he knew, but there were bigger saloons in town, where both gamblers and grifters would find better pickings.

He finished his beer and then went to take a look at his room.

FOUR

The room suited Clint. It was large, well furnished with two dressers and a large bed. He had a feeling it was probably one of the best rooms in the place.

He used the pitcher and basin in the room to clean himself up and then changed into a fresh shirt to go out and find someplace to eat.

He'd been to Bullhead City before, but in those days all the town had to offer was fishing in the Colorado River. It had changed quite a bit since then.

He passed several small cafés and finally stopped at what looked like a busy new restaurant with SPECIAL STEAKS painted on the window.

He went inside and, even though the place was busy, was seated fairly quickly. There was a chalk menu up on the back wall, where everyone could see it.

When the middle-aged waitress came over and asked for his order, he asked, "What's so special about your steaks?"

She smiled, which made her appear a little younger, and said, "Ya gotta order one to find out."

"Okay," he said, "I'll have a special steak."

"Whatcha wanna drink?" she asked.

"What have you got?"

"Water, lemonade, coffee, beer."

"Cold beer?"

"Only kind we got."

"I'll have a beer."

"I'll bring that right out," she promised.

"I'll be right here," he said, and she smiled at him again.

She brought him a huge mug of frosty, frothy beer, better than what he'd had at the saloon. He worked on that, once again checking the room for familiar faces. According to the information he'd been given, there were going to be boxing and wrestling matches, sharpshooting contests, poker tournaments, events on the river, and lots of opportunities for betting, so he knew the town would be filled with gamblers. He expected to start seeing familiar faces in the morning.

The waitress brought his special steak, and it filled the large plate. Onions, carrots, and potatoes shared the platter.

"It looks special," he admitted, picking up his knife and fork.

"If it ain't," she said, "you ain't gotta pay."

"The cook is confident," he said.

"Very," she said. "You let me know if ya want anythin' else."

He took one bite of the steak and knew he wasn't sending it back, and he'd gladly pay for it. It was special in a way he'd never experienced before. There was some kind of crunch on top that he couldn't identify, and he had been to some of the biggest steakhouses in New York and San Francisco. And the vegetables were also prepared to perfection.

He called the waitress over.

"Complaint?" she asked.

"None," he said. "What is this crust on top?"

"Peppercorns," she said. "Do you like it?"

"It's great," he said. "You can give the cook my compliments."

"I'll tell him. Another beer?"

"Definitely," he said.

He was halfway done with his steak when she returned with the beer and a basket of rolls.

"These go real good with the steak," she said. "On the house."

"Thanks."

She was right. They were light and flaky and went real well with the steak.

Folks came and went while he finished his dinner in a leisurely fashion. When the waitress returned, she asked if he wanted dessert.

"If you've got peach pie," he said, "I think I'll be eating here every day while I'm here."

"How long are you gonna be in town?" she asked.

"For as long as the festival lasts."

"Well, I guess we'll be seein' you a lot, then, because we got peach pie."

"Okay," he said. "Bring it out."

"And coffee?"

"Strong and black."

She grinned. "The only way we make it."

Clint was extremely glad he'd passed up some of the smaller, less busy cafes to come to this place. He'd noticed the SPECIAL STEAKS sign in the window and hadn't even bothered to check the name of the place.

He'd have to ask the waitress when she came back with the pie.

FIVE

Clint finished his pie and coffee with equal satisfaction as for the rest of the meal. He hoped he left enough of a tip to make that clear.

He left the restaurant, looked up over the door, and saw the name: CHUCK'S STEAKHOUSE. He assumed Chuck was the owner, and probably the cook.

He started back to the hotel, but since the beer at the steakhouse was better than the beer at the hotel's saloon, he decided to go elsewhere.

He found a larger saloon called the Colorado House Saloon and went inside. As with the Bullhead, it was busy, but it was also three times the size. There were crystal chandeliers hanging from the high ceiling and a balcony running the entire length of the room. The bar was polished dark cherry wood, and smelled very new.

Even though it was busy, there was plenty of room at the impossibly long bar. There were two bartenders at work, both wearing vests, white shirts, and bow ties.

"What can I get ya?" one of them asked.

"Beer."

"Comin' up."

The two barmen were amazingly efficient, and his beer arrived before he knew it.

"Thanks." Beer in hand, he turned to regard the room further. There were gaming tables across the floor, girls in vivid dresses working the floor.

When the bartender came back, Clint sensed his presence, turned, and asked, "How much?"

"I can keep track," the man said. "You can pay before you leave."

"Okay."

"What's your name?"

He hesitated, then said simply, "Clint."

"Okay. Enjoy yourself."

He turned to continue surveying the room. There had to be somebody in this place he knew.

Pushing away from the bar, beer in hand, he started walking around. There was roulette, craps, faro, blackjack and, against the back wall, three poker tables, each with a house dealer.

"'scuse me, sweetie," one of the girls said, brushing by him. She left a lingering scent in her wake that tickled his nose. Another girl whizzed by him, gracing him with a smile and leaving her sweet—but different—scent behind, as well.

The girls were all pretty, their red, blue, green, yellow dresses also revealing lots of smooth skin.

He moved closer to the poker tables, eyeing the players. He didn't see any professional poker players at the first two tables, but spotted a man named Three-Fingered Jack at the third table. He was a gambler Clint had met on several occasions, once or twice across a poker table.

As he watched he recognized another man at the table as a professional. Not that he knew the man, he just recognized his play as being that good.

He watched for about twenty minutes as most of the hands came down to Jack and the other man. When a chair opened up he considered sitting in, but decided against it. He hadn't come to Bullhead City to gamble. He had come as a favor to a friend, who was in turn covering all his expenses. Playing poker was not included in the deal.

In fact, he had to meet with his friend, if not tonight, then in the morning. He had expected the man to be waiting for him at the hotel, so they could discuss things before the festival started.

He walked away from the table, finished his beer, set the mug down on the bar, and left. He headed back to the Bullhead Hotel and Saloon.

"Jesus," Cal Barnes said, "I thought I was gonna have a heart attack when he walked in."

"Never mind," Harry Fields said. "There's no way he can recognize us."

"You don't think he saw us?"

"No," Fields said. "He didn't see us then, and he didn't see us now, so stop worryin'."

"What are we gonna do, though?" Barnes asked.

"We're here for the damn festival, like everybody else," Fields said.

They were sitting at a table together, each with a beer, very close to the batwing doors, so that when Clint walked in they saw him right away.

"Geez," Barnes said, waving to one of the girls, "I need a real drink after that."

"Yeah, okay," Fields said. When the girl came over he said. "Two whiskies, sweetie, okay?"

"Comin' up, boys," she said.

They both watched her walk to the bar and Barnes said, "Damn, she smells sweet."

SIX

When Clint got to the hotel, there was a man waiting in the lobby for him.

"Hey, Clint," Joe Nicholas sand. "Where you been? I've been waitin' here for two hours."

"I needed something to eat," Clint said, "and then a drink, Nicky."

"Yeah, yeah," Nicky said, "I figured. I looked around for you. Where'd you go?"

"Place called Chuck's Steakhouse."

"That dump?" Nicky asked. "I was gonna take you someplace special."

"It was good," Clint said. "I liked it. Besides, you didn't tell me where to find you."

"I know, I was gonna be here to meet you, but I got busy," Nicky said. "It ain't easy puttin' on a festival like this."

"Why would you take on something like this, Nicky?" Clint asked. "You're a gambler, not a showman."

"Maybe I'm lookin' to change," he said. "Look at Cody, and Barnum. They're makin' money hand over fist."

Clint didn't want to tell his friend he wasn't Cody or Barnum. Putting on a festival in Bullhead City just wasn't the same thing.

"How's your room?" Nicky asked. "I got you one of the best in the house."

"It's fine," Clint said. "Comfortable enough."

"Good, good. Look, let's go into the saloon and I'll buy you a drink."

"You're already buying me drinks, and a room," Clint said. "Remember?"

"Yeah, well come on. Let's have another one, on me. We can talk about tomorrow, and the festival."

"Okay, Nicky," Clint said. "Okay."

They got two beers and sat at a back table. A couple of people said hello to Joe Nicholas, but he just waved them off.

"You're already known in town?" Clint asked.

"I been around here a while, getting this set up," Nicky said. "Thanks for agreeing to handle security for me."

"Well, this thing is going to bring lots of the wrong people to town along with the right ones," Clint said.

"How was your ride in?" Nicky asked.

"Eventful," Clint said. "Two jaspers tried to bushwhack me."

"What happened?"

"Nothing much," Clint said. "Nobody got hurt. When I got close to them they took off."

"They tried for you with rifles?"

Clint nodded. "From atop a hill."

"They didn't want any part of you and your gun close up," Nicky said. "I can understand that. Where'd they go?"

"Well, their trail came this way," Clint said. "For all I know, they might be right here in town."

"Well, if they didn't want no part of you out there, they sure won't want any part of you here in town," Nicky said. "I don't think they'll try for you here, but you better watch your back, just in case."

"I always do, Nicky. Hey, I saw Three-Fingered Jack playing poker over at the Colorado Saloon."

"Yeah, Jack's been here a few days. Gettin' warmed up, I guess."

"I saw another pro at the table," Clint said. "Guy in his forties, real sleepy-eyed."

"Sounds like Vince Miles," Nicky said. "He's from back East. He's decided he wants to try his luck with some Western gamblers."

"He was holding his own with Jack," Clint said.

"Jack's not top of the line, Clint," Nicky said. "You know if Bat's comin' in for this?"

"Haven't heard."

"Luke Short?"

"Haven't heard from him, either."

"I need names like that," Nicky said.

"Let's see who shows up, Nicky," Clint said. "Now, who else you got for security?"

"I got who you asked for," Nicky said. "I mean, some of the names you gave me couldn't make it, but others could."

"Like who?"

"I got Billy Jensen and Walt Denver."

"Good boys," Clint said.

"I couldn't get none of the others, though, so I hired two other guys."

"Who?"

"You don't know 'em," Nicky said. "I'll have 'em here in the mornin' for you to meet."

"If I don't like them, Nicky—"

"I know, I know," Nicky said, "we'll let 'em go, but you'll have to hire somebody local if you do that."

"We'll see," Clint said. "The festival starts tomorrow, right?"

"That's right," Nicky said. "Opening festivities down by the river at ten a.m. I'll have all the boys here by nine."

"Good, good. You be here by eight, though. We'll have breakfast together."

"All right."

"What else is happening tomorrow?" Clint asked.

"Wrestling," Nicky said. "That's for the dopes, you know? Next day we'll have the boxing matches. And the sharpshooting event. Then at night, poker."

"Who's entered in the sharpshooting contest?"

"Some locals," Nicky said, "but we still got people signing up tomorrow. I'm expecting the out-of-towners to show up then."

"Okay," Clint said. "You be here with the boys in the morning, and we'll all walk over to the river together."

"I'll see you in the mornin', then," Nicky said, standing up. "I'm really glad you're here, Clint."

"Me, too, Nicky," Clint said. "It's good to see you."

Joe Nicholas walked out. Clint stayed and finished his beer before going to his room.

SEVEN

Clint spent a quiet night in his room, the first one in a while in a real bed. He came down the next morning and met Joe Nicholas in the lobby. They went into the hotel dining room together.

"I haven't eaten in here," Nicky said. "Any good?"

"I don't know," Clint said. "Haven't tried it myself."

"There's a real fine lace in town, do most of my eatin' there," Nicky said. "Sort of like Delmonico's."

"I'm partial to Chuck's," Clint said.

"Well, you gotta try my place."

"I will," Clint said, "if you try mine."

"Deal."

"Right now, I guess we should just try this," Clint said.

A waiter came over, and he ordered steak and eggs. Joe Nicholas asked for the same.

"I talked to the men last night. They'll all be here at nine."

"Maybe we should've had them join us for breakfast," Clint said. "Well, too late now."

"I'm coverin' all your meals, Clint," Nicky pointed out, "but they're gonna have to feed themselves."

"That's fine," Clint said. "I don't need to know your arrangements with them."

"Well, as far as they're concerned, you're the boss," Nicky said. "And they're your men. You do what you want with them."

"Well, I'll pretty much be concerned with breaking up fights, and keeping anybody from stealing anything."

"You mean robbery?"

"I was thinking more about pickpockets. They usually show up when there's a crowd."

"Well," Nicky said, "I'm hopin' there's a crowd."

"You've got no idea how many people you're expecting?" Clint asked.

"Nope," Nicky said. "I just know what I'm hopin' for."

"What about the town fathers?" Clint asked. "They going along with you?"

"The mayor's excited," Nicky said. "So are the storekeepers. They know that they'll all benefit if I can bring a crowd into town."

The waiter came with their plates and set them down.

"Can you bring some more coffee, please?" Clint asked.

"Yes, sir."

"While we eat," Clint said, "why don't you bring me up to date on the mayor, and whoever else you're dealing with? I want to be well informed."

"Okay," Nicky said, "well, the mayor's name is Hudson . . ."

The steak was tough, nowhere near as good as what he'd had at Chuck's Steakhouse.

"That was good," Nicky said, which made Clint wonder

about his friend's taste. Maybe his Delmonico's-style restaurant wouldn't be as good as he claimed.

The coffee was okay, though, and Clint told the waiter to bring some more. They had about ten minutes before the other men were set to show up, but looking out into the lobby from his chair Clint saw Billy Jensen and Walt Denver enter the hotel.

"There's Jensen and Denver," he said. "I'm going to have them come in for some coffee."

"Fine," Nicky said. "I've gotta go, anyway. I'll send them in." He stood up. "The bill's all taken care of."

"Okay, thanks."

Clint watched as Nicky went out to the lobby and spoke to the two men. They looked into the dining room, spotted Clint, and nodded. Nicky left, while Jensen and Denver walked up to Clint's table.

"How are you boys doing?" he asked.

"Pretty good," Denver said.

"Hey, Clint," Jensen said.

"Sit down and have some coffee," Clint said. "The other men should be here soon."

The two men removed their hats and sat down. Clint had the waiter bring four more cups.

"You boys meet the others yet?" Clint asked.

"Yeah, we have," Jensen said.

"They seem okay," Denver said.

"Little raw, maybe."

"Well, one of 'em."

Clint saw that he'd have to judge for himself.

"Well, since you've seen them already, you'll recognize them when they walk in. I'll want to go over the ground rules over coffee when they get here."

"Suits us," Denver said.

"We appreciate the work," Jensen said. "Kinda lean out there these days."

"Can't get the kind of work we used ta get," Jensen said. "This country's changin'."

"Changin' too much," Denver agreed.

Both men were in their early thirties, but Clint had heard their same complaints from older men. The West was changing too much for most westerners. Too much civilization, they said. The railroad was responsible in large part for that, bringing the East closer to the West. Clint would have bet that when East met West, the West would have come out on top, but that wasn't the way things were going. Men like Jensen and Denver, who had made their way with their guns for a long time, were having to find other ways to feed themselves.

Like working security for some fool festival.

"There they are," Jensen said. "I'll get 'em."

"What do you think, Walt?" Clint asked when they were alone.

"The whole thing seems foolish to me, Clint," the man said. "But what're you gonna do? We need the work."

"Shouldn't be hard work, though," Clint said. "Just keep folks from losing their pokes or getting into fights."

"Ain't that what the law's for?"

It occurred to Clint that he and Nicky hadn't spoken about the law—at all.

EIGHT

Just before ten a.m., Clint and his men arrived down by the river, where people had gathered—but certainly not in the numbers Joe Nicholas had been hoping for.

"Okay, fan out," Clint said. "This shouldn't be too hard, nothing really going on yet. Just keep an eye out for pickpockets."

"Okay," Denver said. He and Jensen moved away into the crowd.

The other two men were Will Beck and Dan Hines. Beck was the raw one, probably about twenty-four or so. Hines seemed to be almost thirty.

"What do we do if we see a pickpocket?" Beck asked Clint.

"Just grab him, return the poke if he already got it, and then bring him to me. Got it?"

Beck was going to ask another question but Hines broke in and said, "We got it!"

He pushed Beck ahead of him and the two men melted into the crowd.

* * *

Joe Nicholas was standing at a podium in front of the river, talking to the assembled crowd. He was telling them what they could expect from the coming weeklong Festival. That was actually the first time Clint heard that the festival was a week long. He'd have to mention that to Nicky.

Clint knew that he was sometimes too anxious to help his friends, and that he didn't always ask the right questions. He'd agreed this time because while Bullhead City was not exactly remote, it was off the beaten path. He felt like he could use some time away from the big towns in the West, but while he often spent his down time in Labyrinth, Texas, he sometimes needed to get away from there, as well.

He kept his eyes on the crowd while listening to maybe every third or fourth word coming out of his friend's mouth. The crowd was small enough for him to be able to see his other men moving through, keeping a wary eye open. He wasn't yet sure if Beck and Hines would even be able to spot a pickpocket, but if they couldn't he could always find other things for them to do.

He still didn't see any familiar faces in the crowd. One thing Joe Nicholas's telegram had told him was that he'd be sure to see people he knew. That wasn't the case . . . yet! But he was getting the feeling that this festival wasn't all his friend had led him to believe, and that it was not going to be what Nicholas wanted it to be.

There were some tables set up alongside the podium Nicky was standing on.

"If anyone wants to sign up for any of the events— wrestling, boxing, sharpshooting—just step up to the appropriate table and sign your name."

That was when the crowd broke into factions. Obviously

most of the people who were present were there to sign up for events that had cash prizes. In fact, Clint noticed men signing up for not just one or two events, but all of them. He doubted that someone adept at wrestling would also be good at boxing—and then be able to play poker on top of that. If there was one man present who could do all three of those things well, Clint wanted to meet him.

While people waited in line to sign up, Joe Nicholas came over and stood by Clint.

"I was worried when I didn't see much of a crowd," he admitted, "but it looks like most of them are signing up for an activity."

"Or all three," Clint said.

"Whatever," he said. "The more people who enter, the bigger the prize."

"This is not much of a crowd, Nicky," Clint said. "Plus, I still don't see anybody I know."

"We'll probably get more later in the day," he said. "We're keepin' the tables open so people can sign up late. Did I tell ya, we also got a trick shooter."

"Trick shooter? No, you didn't tell me. Is he allowed to compete in the sharpshooting contest?"

"No," his friend said, "he's getting paid to shoot cigarettes out of people's mouths."

"I'm going to leave the men here by the river to watch while I take a walk through town."

"What are you lookin' for?"

"Known pickpockets, or other troublemakers," Clint said. "By the way, what's the law in this town like?"

"We have the sheriff's cooperation," Nicky said. "The mayor made sure of that."

"What's the sheriff's name?"

"Abernathy," Nicky said. "Not sure of his first name."

"I'll stop in and say hello," Clint said, "let him know I'm in town. Unless he already knows?"

"No." Nicky said. "I didn't tell anybody."

"Why not?"

Nicky shrugged. "It just didn't come up."

"Well," Clint said, "I'll just find out his first name for you."

NINE

Clint walked through Bullhead City, studying the faces of the people he passed along the way. When he got to the sheriff's office, he stopped and knocked on the door.

"Yeah, what!" a man's voice shouted.

Clint opened the door and stepped inside. A man with a badge turned to face him, having just tossed a piece of wood into a stove.

"Can I help ya?" he asked.

"Sheriff Abernathy?"

"That's right," the man said. He was tall: well over six feet, sandy-haired, and very slender.

"My name's Clint Adams, Sheriff," Clint said. "I'm here for the festival."

"That fool thing?" the sheriff asked. "What a waste of time! Wait, did you say Clint Adams?"

"That's right."

"What the hell would a man like you be doin' here for somethin' like this festival?"

"Actually," the Gunsmith said, "I agreed to be responsible for security."

"Again," Abernathy said, "why?"

"The man running the festival asked me to help him."

"That would be Joe Nicholas?"

"That's right."

Abernathy pointed at Clint.

"I don't trust that one. I warned the mayor against agreeing to this."

"What do you have against a festival?"

"It's gonna bring the wrong element to this town," Abernathy said.

"Do you have any deputies?"

"It's a small place," Abernathy said. "There's no need for deputies."

"Well, Joe Nicholas told me he had your cooperation."

Abernathy smiled. "Sure, sure," he said, "I'll cooperate. I told the mayor I would. But that don't mean I'm gonna be part of the fool thing. Might as well have a circus here in town."

Clint couldn't deny that he'd had the same thought himself once or twice this morning. "All right," he said. "I just wanted to introduce myself and let you know I was in town."

"Well . . . I appreciate the courtesy."

Clint left the sheriff's office, figuring the man wouldn't be much help if anything happened. He'd have to count on his own four men.

At first he wasn't sure that four men—and himself—would be enough. But if the crowd didn't get any bigger than this morning's, they'd be more than enough.

He was on his way back to the river when he saw somebody riding into town. First he saw the dark suit and hat, then recognized the way the man sat on his horse. He saw the rider heading toward the Bullhead Hotel and Saloon, and got there first so he was waiting right out front, sitting in a wooden chair.

The rider approached the hotel and, as Clint had hoped, stopped there. He dismounted, looked up at the hotel, then tied his horse off. He removed his saddlebags, tossed them over his shoulder, then grabbed his rifle and stepped up onto the boardwalk.

As the man came up to the door, Clint stood up from his chair. The man stopped and almost went for his gun.

"What the hell are you doing here?" Clint asked Luke Short.

TEN

"I heard you were gonna be here," Short said to Clint. It was about twenty minutes later. Short had registered at the hotel, dropped his gear in his room, and they were in the saloon, each with a beer.

"Where'd you hear that?"

"Joe Nicholas sent me a telegram."

"He sent me one, too," Clint said. "Asked me to handle security. What did he ask you?"

"Just to come," Luke Short said. "He said I might find some of my friends here, but that you would definitely be in town."

"So you came?"

"Is there gonna be poker?" Short asked.

"Well, yeah . . ."

"So I came. Don't think it had anythin' to do with seein' you."

"Don't worry," Clint said, "I won't."

"Is Bat here?" Short asked.

"No, and I don't know that he's coming."

"Anybody else we know here?"

"Three-Fingered Jack."

"Anybody else?"

"Guy named Vince Miles. Know him?"

"Never heard of him. How many people have come to town for this thing?"

"Doesn't look like that many."

"Joe's telegram said there'd be plenty of opportunity to make money."

"I think he left out 'he hoped,'" Clint said.

"Well, what's supposed to happen at this thing?" Short asked.

"Wrestling, boxing, poker, stuff on the river," Clint said. "Oh, and there's a trick shooter."

"That should be interesting." Short rolled his eyes.

"Yeah."

"You want to work while you're here?" Clint asked.

"Doin' what?"

"Security."

Short scowled.

"Just spotting pickpockets," Clint said, "breaking up fights—"

"Gunfights?"

"I hope not."

Short made a face again. "Bet it pays horseshit."

"You got that right."

"Never mind, then," Short said. "I'll see what I can make on my own."

"Well, if you go over to the Colorado Saloon you might find Jack or that fellow Miles at one of the tables."

"First I want a bath," Short said. "And I need to change my clothes and get this suit cleaned."

"Dapper Luke," Clint said. "Well, I'll be around, probably down by the river, where a lot of this is supposed to take place."

"What's across the river?" Luke asked.

"Not much," Clint said. "We're downriver of Laughlin, Nevada."

"Never been there."

"I have," Clint said. "It's small, not much going on there."

"Okay," Short said, standing up. "Thanks for the beer. I'll catch up to you later, down by the river."

"Watch your back, Luke," Clint said. "The sheriff here isn't going to be much help."

"What else is new?" Short asked. He didn't have much respect for most lawmen—except his own friends like Wyatt Earp and Bat Masterson.

Clint walked out to the lobby with Short, and then they parted ways. Clint walked back down to the river to check on his boys.

ELEVEN

Clint saw that people were still signing up to compete in the wrestling, boxing, and sharpshooting matches. He looked around for Joe Nicholas, but didn't see him. Then he looked for his men but only saw one: Walt Denver, standing by one of the tables, apparently refereeing an argument between a woman and the man seated at the table. Other people were gathering around to watch and listen.

". . . . don't see why not," the woman was saying as Clint approached. "Show me a written rule."

"What's going on, Walt?" Clint asked.

"This lady is trying to sign up for the boxing matches, and this fella won't let her."

"Okay," Clint said, "I'll handle it. Move these other people along."

"Sure, Clint."

Clint went to the table, said to the seated man, "What's the problem?"

"I'll tell you what the problem is—" the woman started, turning to face him. When she saw him, she stopped. He was first struck by her height—better than six feet. Then he saw her face. Not beautiful, but striking—the kind of face you caught yourself staring at, and remembering for a long time later. Her hair was so blonde it was almost white, and the same went for her eyebrows, which you had to look close to see. Her eyes were sea blue, and large.

"She wants to sign up for the boxing matches," the man at the table said.

"And?"

"Well . . . she's a woman!" The man stared at Clint like he was crazy for having to explain.

"I wanna see a rule. In writing," the woman said. "A rule that says I can't box."

Clint looked at her again.

"Are you sure you want to do this, miss?"

"I am," she said. "I can whip any man." She jabbed him in the chest with her forefinger. "I can whip you."

"I believe you," he said, "but I'm not in the matches. I assume a lot of big men are."

"It don't matter the size," she said.

Clint looked at the man. "You got a written rule?"

"No, but—"

"So let her sign up."

"But—"

"You know who I am?"

"Yessir, Mr. Nicholas told all of us volunteers who you are."

"Then do it. Let her sign up."

The man, beefy, in his fifties, shrugged and said, "Okay. It's her funeral."

Clint turned to the woman.

"Okay?"

"Yeah, sure," she said. "Thanks."

"Still want to whip me?"

"Well, no," she said, "sorry about that. My name's Brenda Mitchell."

"My name's Clint Adams," he said. "I'll have to come and watch you fight."

"I'd like that."

"Can you write?" the seated man asked.

"Of course I can write!" she snapped.

"Sign here, then."

While the woman leaned over to sign Clint walked away, still looking for his other men.

"Hey, mister!" the woman called.

He turned. She came walking over to him. Behind her the man sitting at the table was shaking his head, but he was still watching her walk away.

"You done me a favor," she said. "I'd like to buy you a drink."

"I don't know if I did you a favor," he said, "but I'll take the drink if we can do it later."

"Sure, when?"

"How about tonight, at the Colorado Saloon. After seven?"

"Sure thing," she said. "Meanwhile, could you tell me where to get a good steak?"

"I sure can," he said. "Place called Chuck's Steakhouse." He gave her directions.

"Much obliged," she said. "Gotta keep my strength up. I'll see you later at the saloon."

"I'm looking forward to it," Clint said.

He watched her walk off. She was a big woman, but he still found her feminine and appealing. He wondered how he'd feel about her if he watched her box a man . . . and win!

He looked around, saw other men watching her walk away, as well.

TWELVE

Clint found his men. Billy Jensen was holding a ten-year-old boy by the scruff of the neck and going through his pockets.

"What have we here?" he asked.

"I saw him dip his hand into one man's pocket," Jensen said. "I'm sure it wasn't the first."

"Well, if you find any wallets hang onto them," Clint said. "Same for any money."

"Hey, that's mine!" the boy shouted as Jensen took a few coins from his pocket.

"Sure," Jensen said.

"I picked some pockets, but those coins are mine!" the boy said again.

"We'll see about that." Jensen pocketed the coins, looked to Clint. "Should I take him to the sheriff?"

"Let him go," Clint said. The boy's face brightened. "But if you find him dipping again, bite his hand off at the wrist."

"What?" the boy said, shocked.

"That's what pickpockets deserve," Clint said. "That and a kick in the pants!"

Jensen let the boy go and he started running, but not before Clint delivered the kick.

"Go home and stay there!" he shouted.

"Where are the other two?" he asked Jensen. "Beck and Hines."

"I ain't seen 'em since this mornin'," Jensen said. "Walt stayed down by the river."

"I saw him there," Clint said. "Find the other two. If they're not doing their jobs, I'll fire their asses on the spot."

"Okay, Clint."

"I'll keep looking, as well," Clint said. "Also for Joe Nicholas."

"I'll tell him if I see him," Jensen said.

"Nice job, spotting the boy."

"Thanks," Jensen said. "Do you think we scared him enough?"

"I doubt it," Clint said. "He probably supports his family with what he steals."

"If that's the case," Jensen said, taking coins from his pocket, "you better see he gets these back."

"That's more than you took off him."

"Yeah," Jensen said, "it is."

Clint walked the rest of the town, didn't come across either Beck or Hines. But he did finally cross paths with Joe Nicholas, coming out of a brick building as Clint was passing.

"There you are," he said.

Nicholas looked at him in surprise, then pointed at the building he'd just exited.

"City Hall," he said. "I was just talkin' to the mayor."

"About what?"

"Details," Nicholas said. "Last-minute details."

"Well, here are some details for you. I can't find Beck or Hines, and you have a woman signed up to compete in the boxing matches."

"A what?"

"A woman," Clint said.

"What idiot let that happen?"

"That would be my doing," Clint said. "Apparently, you have no written rules against it."

"By God," Nicholas said. "The first blow will kill her."

"I doubt it," Clint said. "You didn't see her."

"I better get back to the river, before they let a blind man sign up." Nicholas started away, then stopped. "Unless you'd agree to that since there's no written rule against it?"

"You know," Clint said, "that might be interesting, at that."

"Jesus," Nicholas said, shaking his head.

Clint spent the rest of the afternoon looking for his two men, and not finding them. As far as he was concerned, they were already fired.

When he got back to the river Nicholas was there, as well as Luke Short.

"You find them?" Nicholas asked.

"No," Clint said. "If you see them, tell them they're already fired."

"Maybe Luke here will work security."

"I already asked him," Clint said. "There's not enough money in it for him."

"I'll pay him what I was payin' both of them," Nicholas said, looking over at Short, who was resplendent in a clean suit.

"Won't matter," Clint said. "It's not enough."

"What if you asked him to do it as a favor?" Nicholas asked.

"To you?"

"No, to you."

Clint shook his head. "I'm here as a favor to you," he said. "I won't ask Luke to do the same for me. Not in this instance. Jensen, Walt, and I will have to do the best we can."

"Okay," Nicholas said. "Hey, what was that woman's name who signed to box? Brenda somethin'?"

"Mitchell," Clint said. "Ever hear of her?"

"No, but Bud—he signed her—said she was good looking. A large woman, but good looking."

"She was that," Clint said. "An interesting woman."

"No wonder you let her sign."

"Well," Clint said, "she did say she wanted to buy me a drink."

"Better get to her, then, before she gets into the ring," Nicholas advised. "Pretty girls ain't so pretty with a broken nose."

THIRTEEN

Clint was in the Colorado Saloon at seven-twenty, standing at the bar when Brenda Mitchell walked in. She attracted some attention for several reasons. One, she was a woman walking into a saloon. Two, she was a large woman walking into a saloon. Three, she was an attractive woman walking into a saloon.

She didn't seem to notice, though. She looked around, spotted Clint at the bar, and walked over. She was wearing jeans, and boots that made her over six feet. In fact, she appeared to be about an inch taller than he was. She had a hat behind her head, hanging from a string. If she'd been wearing it, she would have seemed a lot taller than he was.

"Mr. Adams."

"Miss Mitchell," he said. "Maybe you should just call me Clint."

"I'm Brenda," she said. "Beer?"

"Don't mind if I do."

She waved at the bartender, who came over and said, "Wow. What'll ya have, miss?"

"Two beers."

"Comin' up."

He drew two beers, set them in front of her, then stood and stared.

"Go away," she said.

"Yes, ma'am." He looked at Clint. "Good luck."

They each picked up their beer and had a sip.

"Where's your room?" she asked.

"The Bullhead."

"How many beers we gonna have before we go there and fuck?"

He'd known a lot of women in his time, but only a handful had surprised him. Brenda had just made the list.

"Is one too many?" he asked.

She grinned at him. If she was actually a boxer, she must have been pretty good at it. Her nose wasn't broken and never had been, and she had all her teeth. And no facial scars.

"What, too direct?" she asked.

"Just for a minute," he said. "I just had to figure out whether you were kidding or not."

"And what did you decide?"

"I don't know," he said. "I guess I'll find out when we get to my room."

They drank some more beer.

"Tell me about yourself," he said.

"Whaddaya wanna know?"

"How long have you been boxing?"

"A year."

"Against men?"

"Yeah."

"You sure you want to get into the ring with men who have been doing it a lot longer?"

"Makes me fresher," she said. "You were lookin' at my face. You can tell I'm good because I'm still so pretty." She touched her own face. "I got real smooth skin."

"And amazing eyes."

"Why, thank you, sir." She finished her beer. "If you're a bettin' man, you better put it all on me."

"What've you got that they don't?" he asked.

"I'm fast," she said, "and I can't be hit."

"Can you hit?"

"Oh, yes."

"This is going to be with gloves, you know."

She shrugged.

"Gloves, bare-knuckle, it don't much matter to me." She put her empty mug on the bar. "I'm ready."

He finished his beer and put the mug on the bar.

"You're not going to hurt me, are you?" he asked.

She grinned. "I guess we'll find out when we get to your room."

FOURTEEN

Luke Short looked over at the bar from his seat at the poker table and saw Clint with the tall girl. He figured this must be the girl he'd told Luke about, the one who wanted to box against men. Imagine the odds, he thought, if she really could beat a man.

"Looks like your friend Adams has made a new friend," Three-Fingered Jack said.

Short looked across the table at Jack. He never understood how the man got his name. He had all his fingers.

"Guess he's not gonna be playin', huh?"

"Not poker, anyway," Short said. "You call, or what?"

"Oh, I call, Luke," Jack said. "I call."

"So do I," Vince Miles said.

Jack looked at him. "I forgot you were in this hand," he said.

Miles smiled. "That's okay," he said. "I'll make sure you always remember I'm here."

Short had watched the game a while before sitting down to play. It was clear that Miles and Jack had been going at each other for some time. He thought it was a situation he could take advantage of.

"Full house," he said, spreading his cards.

"Beats me," Jack said.

"Me, too," Miles said.

Short raked in his chips, wondering how much of this money he should bet on the girl boxer. After he'd heard from Clint if she was any good, of course.

When they entered his room, she walked around slowly, looking it over.

"Nice," she said. "You got the money to pay for a room like this?"

"It's free," he said.

"Oh, because you're workin' the festival?" she asked. "As what?"

"Security."

"If you're security, why'd you get involved in my dispute?" she said. "I wasn't gonna hurt anybody."

"Well," he said with a smile, "I didn't know that."

She walked up to him, stood toe to toe, chest to chest. He kissed her, tilting his chin up slightly.

"Uh, can you take off the boots?" he asked.

She smiled. "Tall women intimidate you?"

"Not if they're really taller than me," he said. "With you, it's the boots. How tall are you without them?"

"Five-foot-eleven." She backed off a few feet, took the hat from around her neck, and tossed it aside. Then she sat on the bed and tugged at her boots.

"A little help?" she asked.

He stood with his back to her, bent over, and took her leg and boot between his legs. He grabbed on; she put her other foot against his butt and pushed, and her boot came off. He grabbed the other foot. This time, she put her foot against his butt and he could feel the heat from her foot.

"Nice butt," she said, rubbing it with her foot.

"Want me to get this other boot?"

She pressed her foot against his ass and pushed. The second boot slid off.

"Socks?" she said. "Please?"

He took off her first sock, then the second. He held onto her foot, though, and rubbed it. No calluses from wearing boots all the time; her skin was very smooth.

"Pretty feet," he said.

She pulled her foot free and said, "I'm pretty all over, which you're gonna find out."

He stood up straight, turned, and faced her. She was reclining on her elbows, one foot bent, regarding him with a smile.

"So," he said, "show me."

"Uh-uh," she said. She pointed with her foot and said, "You first."

"Not in a hurry, huh?"

"That's the benefit of having sex sober," she said. "No rushing."

He removed his gun belt and hung it on the bedpost.

"I have to have sex with a gun hanging over my head?" she asked.

"Sorry," he said. "I need it to be within reach."

"Oh, that's right," she said. "You're the Gunsmith."

He stood next to the bed, looking down at her. She swiveled around to face him, pressing her bare foot against his crotch. She could feel his hard column of flesh through the denim.

"Hey," she said, "interested already?"

"I've been interested since I first saw you this morning," he said.

"Oh," she said, "you poor man. Is it painful?"

"Not yet."

She rubbed him with her foot.

"Okay," he said, "getting there."

She removed her toes from the front of his jeans. "Then continue to undress, sir."

FIFTEEN

Joe Nicholas sat at a table in a small saloon known only as Saloon #8. It was in a run-down section of Bullhead City, which the town fathers had been promising to clean up. Until they kept that promise, it was a good place to find men who would do a job for pay—any job, as long as the pay was good.

He was nursing a bottle of whiskey, waiting for a man who was supposed to meet him there half an hour ago.

It was full dark out. The festival had been put to bed for the day. Tomorrow it would begin again in earnest with wrestling matches, and a trick shot demonstration.

The man Nicholas was waiting for had made certain promises, and he was waiting to see if those promises were going to be kept.

Even nursing the bottle, he'd drunk a third of it by the time the man arrived.

"You leave any for me?" Rusty Cooper asked, sitting opposite Nicholas.

"You kept me waiting half an hour," Nicholas said. "What was I supposed to do, just stare at the bottle?"

Cooper pushed an empty glass over to Nicholas and said, "Pour me some."

Nicholas did so, mostly because he was afraid. The man was deadlier than most because he was crazy.

"What's goin' on?" Cooper asked.

"I had a talk with the mayor today," Nicholas said. "He's talkin' about not payin'."

"He agreed."

"I know, I told him that," Nicholas said. "But he says we ain't deliverin' what we said we would."

"Tell him not to worry," Cooper said. "They'll come."

"What makes you so sure?"

"I got word circulatin'," Cooper said. "Once it gets around, they'll come."

"What if they don't come soon enough?"

"We got a week," Cooper said, grabbing the bottle and pouring another drink for himself. "You're too nervous."

"I don't like usin' Clint this way," Nicholas said.

"Zat so?" Cooper asked. "Why don't you tell him, then?"

"Are you crazy?" Nicholas asked. He was immediately sorry he had used that word, but it didn't seem to bother Cooper, who chuckled.

"That's what some people say about me, isn't it?" he asked. "That I'm crazy? Well, we'll see."

"What about the trick shooter?" Nicholas asked. "Is he in town?"

"He's here," Cooper said. "He'll be ready."

"How good is he?"

"He's real good."

"Fast?"

"Accurate," Cooper said. "And probably fast—but I could kill him."

"How do you figure?" Nicholas asked. "You don't have a rep as a fast gun."

"It ain't who's fastest, Joey," Cooper said. He was the only person who called Nicholas that, rather than "Nicky," which the man preferred. "This kid can plug an ace of spades at a hundred feet, but he ain't never faced another man with a gun. It ain't an easy thing to do. He's a target shooter, nothing more."

"Well, that don't matter," Nicholas said, "because that's all we want him to do, shoot targets."

"Yeah, well, that he can do real well," Cooper answered. The man finished his second drink and pushed the glass away.

"Don't get nervous on me, Joey," he said.

"Hard not to get nervous with the Gunsmith in town," Nicholas said.

"I thought you guys were friends."

"We are, kinda," Nicholas said.

"So whaddaya worried about?"

"That don't mean Clint Adams likes bein' used," Nicholas said.

"Then he don't have to know."

"What if he finds out?"

"I can take care of Adams," Cooper said, "if it comes to that. Don't worry."

"How would you do that?"

"Just remember what I said," Cooper replied, standing up. "It ain't always the fastest gun who wins. I'll see you tomorrow. Same time."

Cooper turned and walked out of the saloon.

Nicholas grabbed the bottle and poured himself another stiff drink. Getting hooked up with Rusty Cooper might end up being the worst mistake of his life.

SIXTEEN

Brenda watched as Clint removed his clothes. When he was naked, he stood in front of her, his painful erection straining toward her.

"Oh my," she said. She leaned forward, took it in her hand, and stroked it a bit. "You are a pretty man, aren't you?"

"I'm getting a little long in the tooth to be called pretty," he said.

"I ain't talkin' about your face," she said. She flicked the head of his penis with her thumb, then stroked the underside, making it jump.

He slapped her hand away and said, "Your turn to show."

He reached out and gave her his hands, then pulled her to her feet. He kissed her soundly first, then turned her around and took her place on the bed so he could watch.

"Well," she said, "if I must, I must."

She started to unbutton her shirt, pulled it free from her pants. She removed it tantalizingly slow until her breasts—big, round, dark-tipped—came into view.

"How can you box with those things bouncing around inside your shirt?" he asked.

"I tie them down."

He shook his head.

"That's a crime."

She cupped her breasts in her own hands, flicked her nipples with her thumb.

"Cut that out!" he said.

She laughed, removed the rest of her clothes, and then stood with her hands on her hips.

"That's it," he said. "I can't wait any more. Come here."

She moved to the bed, crawled onto it, and straddled him. He tried to pull her down so he could get to her breasts with his mouth, but she playfully fought him. She was extremely strong, but eventually he either broke her or she gave in, and he was able to get those brown nipples into his mouth. He punished her by biting them, but it only made her moan with pleasure.

He ran his hands over her, enjoying the way her muscles felt beneath her toned, smooth flesh. She rubbed her bushy pubic patch up and down the length of his penis, wetting him with her juices.

He pulled her down so he could kiss her, ran his hands down her back to cup her ass. She shifted her hips and suddenly, he was inside her. She was so hot and wet, he slid into her almost before either of them knew it.

But now she was aware, and she caught her breath and sat straight up on him.

"Oh, yes," she said, grinding herself down onto him. "God, you feel so deep."

She closed her eyes and just moved on him, gently at first, and then not so much faster, but harder. She raised herself up and then brought herself down on him, effectively ramming him into her so that they both grunted.

He continued to run his hands over her smooth skin, rubbed her nipples with his palms and his fingers. The brown of her nipples was in stark contrast to the paleness of her skin. They were larger, longer than most nipples he'd ever seen. He squeezed them between his fingers as she continued to ride him.

Her breath started to come in gasps as her body grew tense.

"Oh god," she said, "oh my." She opened her eyes wide as a wave of pleasure washed over her, then bit her lips as she rode it out.

He waited until he felt her body relax, then surprised her by lurching up, bucking her off, and putting her on her back. He got between her legs again, rammed himself into her, and began pounding away, looking for his own release, this time . . .

Rusty Cooper entered the Colorado Saloon, claimed a place at the bar, and ordered himself a drink. From across the room he could see the poker table with Luke Short, Three-Fingered Jack, and Vince Miles.

He relaxed with his beer, waited for Miles to look over at him, then jerked his head. He saw the gambler excuse himself from the table and come over to the bar.

"Bartender, beer, please," Miles said.

The bartender brought it over, said, "One of the girls woulda brung it to ya, Mr. Miles."

"That's okay," Miles said, "I needed to take a walk."

He stood next to Cooper and the two men talked without seeming to talk, so that no one would notice they were having a conversation.

"Nicholas is gettin' nervous," Cooper said.

"Did you calm him down?"

"Yeah, I think so."

"What's he nervous about?"

"Adams."

"You tell him you'll take care of Adams?"

"Yeah, don't you start to worry," Cooper said. "I'll handle it."

"You shouldn't be in here, if Short knows you," Miles said.

"He's seen me a time or two, but he don't know me."

"I've got to get back to the game," Miles said. "If you have to drink tonight, do it somewhere else, will you?"

"Sure, sure," Cooper said. "Just let me finish this one."

He watched as Miles carried his beer back to the table with him. That's all he needed, everybody getting nervous on him.

That was why he usually worked alone, so he wouldn't have to worry about anybody else's emotions. If a plan went wrong, he always preferred to be able to blame himself, not somebody else.

He finished his beer, wiped his mouth with the back of his hand, and—with a last look over at the poker table—headed for the batwings.

SEVENTEEN

Later, Clint had Brenda flipped over onto her stomach, and was exploring the miles of tender flesh that made up her back. He traced the line of her spine with his mouth, and when he reached the cleft between her buttocks he licked the salty sweat from there. She wriggled as he moved his mouth lower, kissing the backs of her thighs, the tender spots behind her knees. Her legs were so long it took him a while to get to her feet. By the time he did, his erection was raging again.

He spread her legs and knelt between them, slid his hand beneath her, palming her belly, rubbing it, then sliding his hand to her wet crotch. He had intended to massage her until she was ready, but this woman seemed to be wet and ready all the time. He lifted her onto all fours, moved up behind her, and slid his dick up between her thighs and into her. She caught her breath and arched her back. He grabbed her long blonde hair and rode her like she was a bronc he was trying to break . . .

* * *

"You know what I really liked?" she asked later, as they lay side by side.

"What?"

"When you pulled my hair."

"Really?"

"Oh yeah," she said. "I've never been manhandled that way before. I think it's because men are intimidated by my size."

"Well, I don't find your size intimidating," he said, "I find it exciting."

She slid her hand down his belly to his cock and said, "I find you exciting, too. I think when I'm in the ring, beating a man senseless, you'll find that exciting, too."

"Oh," he said, "well, I'll let you know."

"Um, I guess I should've mentioned this before," she said, "but I don't have anyplace to stay tonight."

"No hotel room?"

"Nope."

"Stable."

"I can't sleep on hay."

"I was kidding," he said. "You'll sleep here, of course."

"Well," she said, closing her hand over him, "I guess we could sleep . . . in between . . ."

"Don't you need to rest before you fight?"

"Don't worry," she said. "I'll get some rest, but you might not."

She was right. She didn't give him much rest, and when she slept he didn't seem to be able to. His heart was beating too fast.

The woman was trying to give him a heart attack. As proof, when he finally fell asleep he woke with his dick in her mouth. She had started while he was asleep, and he was fully hard when he woke. She sucked him avidly, using her hands as well, until he exploded into her mouth with a loud yell.

He actually fell back asleep after that, but it wasn't long before sunlight was streaming in the window.

In the morning, she got dressed while he watched. He figured he could get an hour's sleep after she left.

"Are you gonna come and watch me fight?" she asked.

"Sure," he said. "What time?"

"Somehow," she said, "I ended up being the first fight of the day. Nine a.m. My guess is they want to see me get knocked out early."

So, no hour's sleep. "Could that happen?"

She smiled. "Not early," she said. "Not at all."

"I'll be there," he promised. "Do you know who you're fighting?"

"No."

"Don't you need to know so you can prepare?"

"I prepare the same for every fight," she said. She came to the bed and kissed him hard. "I gotta go get my gloves," she said. "I'll see you down by the river. They're erecting an outdoor ring to be used for wrestling and boxing."

"I'll see you soon," he said.

She went out the door on the run.

He rolled over, closed his eyes, then opened them wide. The woman was a big, strong boxer. If he fell asleep and missed her match, there was no telling what she might do to him.

She might even make sure he never had sex with her again.

He jumped out of bed.

EIGHTEEN

Clint found Joe Nicholas down by the river, next to the newly erected ring.

"I thought you were going to have the wrestling first?" he asked.

"And miss a chance to see this girl get knocked out?" Nicholas asked. "I want to start the day out right."

In one corner, Brenda's opponent, a large, raw-boned man in his forties, was swinging at the air like he was swatting flies with his gloves. He had a robe over his shoulders, and another man with him.

"Are there rules?" Clint asked.

"Of course," Nicholas said. "Marquess of Queensberry rules . . . kinda."

"What do you mean, kinda?"

"Well, I couldn't find a referee who actually knew all the rules, so . . ."

Brenda appeared and climbed into the ring. No robe, nobody else with her. She had boxing gloves on, and he could see that beneath her shirt she had bound her breasts so they wouldn't be in her way. She had also braided her hair.

She stood in her corner, perfectly still, staring across at her opponent, who was a lot bigger.

The referee got into the ring next. He looked like a sober version of the town drunk.

People began to arrive, and Clint was surprised at the size of the crowd.

"We spread the word that we had a woman boxing a man," Nicholas said. "Figured it would attract attention."

So that was why they had moved the fight up to nine a.m. Nicholas figured once the crowd was there they'd stay.

Clint looked around, saw Luke Short on one side of the ring. Billy Jensen and Walt Denver were already working the crowd.

"Who are the judges?" Clint asked.

"What judges?" Nicholas asked.

"Who's scoring the fight?"

"Nobody."

"I thought you said Marquess of—"

"I said kinda," Nicholas said.

"So how do you know who wins?"

"When he knocks her out," Nicholas said, with a grin, "he wins."

"And what about if *she* knocks *him* out?"

"That ain't gonna happen."

Clint couldn't stop himself. The words were out of his mouth before he could stop them.

"Want to bet?"

A few minutes later, he walked over to where Luke Short was standing.

"There you are," Short said. "Come on, fill me in. I want to make a bet."

"On the man?"

"That's not where the odds are," Short said.

"You're going to bet on her?"

"Only if you tell me she has a chance," Short said.

Clint remembered the strength he'd felt in bed. It was certainly no way to judge a fighter, but . . .

"She strong, and she's fast," he said.

"So she has a chance?" Short asked. "I should bet on her?"

Clint's reply was evasive. "I already bet on her," he said.

"Good enough for me," Short said.

He went away, came back in a few minutes. "I'm gonna make a killing," Short said.

"Who'd you bet with?" Clint asked.

"They've got somebody takin' bets for the festival."

"I hope you were careful," Clint said.

"Careful?" Short asked. "Whoever made money bein' careful?"

Clint looked at his friend. "Luke, how much did you bet?"

"All of it," Short said. "I bet it all."

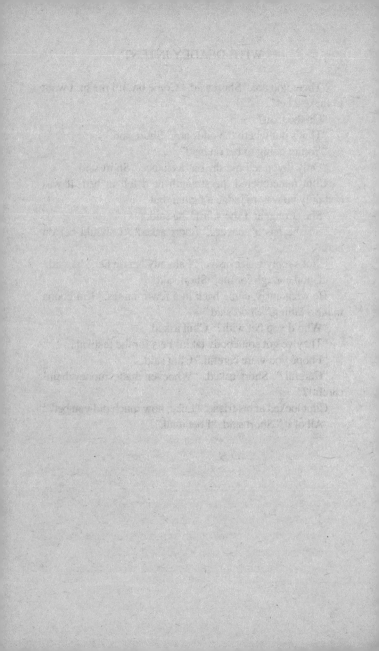

NINETEEN

Clint was worried.

He was worried that Brenda would get hurt.

He was worried that Luke Short was going to lose all his money.

He just hoped Brenda was as good as she seemed to think she was.

He caught her eye that moment and, as if she knew what he was thinking, she winked at him.

Joe Nicholas climbed into the ring and waved at the crowd for their attention.

"I'm your host, Joe Nicholas," he called out. "Allow me to introduce the combatants. In this corner," he said, pointing at the man, "standing five-ten and weighing two hundred and twenty pounds, Killer Kendall. And in this corner, standing five-foot-eleven and weighing one hundred and seventy-six pounds, Brenda 'the Bomb' Mitchell."

Brenda the Bomb. Clint wondered who had come up with that name.

"Seconds out of the ring," Nicholas called.

The other man with Kendall left the ring. Brenda had no second. Clint felt bad, like he should have gotten into the ring with her.

Nicholas had even gotten a bell, and had somebody ready to ring it. He pointed, and the bell rang.

Round one.

Clint watched the proceedings with great interest. Kendall came out of his corner swinging. He swung five times and missed all five. And yet Brenda seemed to have not moved very much.

She was fast!

Finally, she threw a punch, a jab that hit Kendall square on the nose.

Whap!

It was hard, and blood flowed from his nose right away. That one punch brought the crowd right over to her side.

With blood covering the lower part of his face, Kendall waded in with both arms swinging. He missed every punch. And every time he missed, she made him pay. Whap! Whap-whap! Whapwhapwhap!

She never used her right hand, only left jabs.

The bell rang for the end of the first round and Kendall wobbled back to his corner. He sat down on his stool while his second—trainer, manager, whatever—cleaned the blood off his face and screamed into it at the same time.

Brenda went to her corner, stood and waited, relaxed against the ropes.

It went on like that for three more rounds, and then she threw the right. Clint didn't know if the punch was that powerful, or if Kendall was just weak from blood loss, but he fell onto his back and just lay there.

Everybody fell quiet while the referee counted to ten. And then somebody whooped and hollered.

It was Luke Short.

Brenda climbed out of the ring. She had lots of Kendall's blood on her shirt, but she didn't seem to notice.

Clint went over to meet her as she stepped down. She smiled at him. She was sweating, but was not breathing hard. She had been breathing harder the night before while they were having sex.

"Was I right?" she asked with a smile.

"You were right," he said. "You can beat a man."

"No," she said, "I mean the other thing."

"What other thing?"

She leaned forward and said in his ear, "That you'd get excited watching me fight?"

She felt his crotch, and even through her boxing glove— which was basically just a thin layer of leather—she could feel he was hard.

"Ha!" she said. "Do you wanna go and fuck?"

The idea of fucking her while she was all sweaty from the ring appealed to him in an odd way.

"I do," he said, "but I have to work."

"Then I'm gonna go take a bath," she said.

But before she could walk away, Joe Nicholas was there.

"That was great!" he said to her. "That was fantastic."

"When's my next fight?"

"Tomorrow night," he said. "You're not fightin' in the mornin' anymore."

"Good," she said. "That means I can sleep late."

"I've got big plans for you," he said. "Do you have somebody?"

"Somebody?" she asked.

"A manager. A trainer." he said. "Somebody I can do business with."

"Um, yeah I do," she said.

"Good. Who?" Nicholas asked.

She pointed at Clint, said, "Him," and went to take her bath.

TWENTY

"What is she talkin' about?" Joe Nicholas asked. "You're representin' her?"

"I guess so."

"But you work for me."

"I can do both," Clint said. "Don't worry, I'll still handle security. What are you worried about? It's not like you're paying her. She's fighting for the festival."

"But I could make a lot of money off her," Nicholas said.

"After what people just saw?" Clint asked. "Word's going to get around, Nicky."

"Yeah, but the guy she beat was a bum," Nicholas said. "Believe me, we can still get great odds on her in her next fight."

"Which is against who?"

"Whoever wins this fight," Nicholas said.

Clint looked into the ring, saw two young fighters who looked as if they had been cut from granite. Nicholas got into the ring to introduce them. They were each in their twenties, and weighed better than 250 pounds.

The fight began, and went on for thirteen rounds, the two men pounding each other. Finally, one of them could take no more and fell.

"The winner," Nicholas announced, "Matt 'the Mauler' Stuart."

When Nicholas came out of the ring, Clint said, "Why isn't the Mauler wrestling?"

"He is," Nicholas said. "He's competing in both events."

"You expect Brenda to fight him?"

"You see? That's what everyone is gonna think. We can get great odds on her!"

"And what if she doesn't win?"

Nicholas frowned.

"You're handling her," he said. "You don't think she can win?"

"She probably can, if she can avoid getting hit even once," Clint said.

"Well, you tell her that," Nicholas said.

"Yeah, I'll tell her," Clint said.

Nicholas walked away, rubbing his palms together, and stopped to talk to the Mauler.

Luke Short came over to Clint with a handful of money he was counting.

"Clint, my boy," he said, "that was great! I made a killing!"

"Good for you."

"Who does she fight next? And when?"

"Tomorrow night," Clint said, "she fights the winner of this fight."

"That fella?" Short asked. "The Mauler?"

"That's him."

Short frowned thoughtfully. "Hmm, I'd still get great odds on her, but can she beat him?"

"I don't know, Luke."

"Well, ask her, boy," Short said, "ask her."

Nicholas had set up temporary bath facilities in tents down by the river for any wrestlers or boxers who wanted to take a bath.

Clint walked over, caught Brenda walking out of the tent wrapped in a towel, but still showing plenty of flesh. When she saw him, she lowered the towel so that her breasts jutted into view, and then began to rub them.

"Boy, sure hurts tying these girls down," she said.

"Well, you better cover them up," he said, pulling the towel up. "Out here, you'll drive somebody to distraction— or worse. In fact, why don't you get dressed?"

"That's not somethin' a girl wants to hear from her lover," she said.

"Well, I'm not here as your lover," he said. "I'm here as your . . . your second."

"Is that right?"

They walked around to the side of the tent so that they were standing between two tents, where she had left her clothes. She started to get dressed.

"You didn't see the fight I just saw," he said. "Two huge young fighters just pummeled each other until one of them fell down. The winner is called 'the Mauler,' and he weighs two hundred and seventy pounds."

"Why are you tellin' me this?"

"Because he's your next opponent!" Clint said. "What kind of chance do you have against somebody like that?"

"He may be big and strong," she said, "but he still has to hit me to beat me. If I was you, I'd take the odds and bet big—on me!"

TWENTY-ONE

Clint met Luke Short at the Colorado Saloon for a drink, and then they were going to get lunch at Chuck's Steakhouse. He figured Jensen and Denver could handle the security details, since the crowd numbers had still not swelled to dangerous proportions.

The each ordered a beer and then Short asked, "So what about it? Should I let it ride?"

"I'd make a bet, but be cautious, Luke," Clint said.

"You don't make money bein' cautious, Clint," Short said. "You know that as well as I do."

"If you bet it all and lose, you'll be broke."

"I've been broke before," Short said. "You just start over again. What'd the girl say?"

"She said to bet it all on her."

"Okay, then," Short said. "That's good enough for me. Are you gonna bet?"

"Yes, but I'm not the gambler you are," Clint said. "I'll bet a little less."

Short drank some beer and then said, "Now, you and this girl, is there anything . . . else goin' on?"

"Anything else?" Clint said, feigning ignorance.

"You know what I mean," Short said. "There shouldn't be any of that before a fight for a boxer. Takes out the legs, you know?"

"I didn't see anything wrong with her legs this morning," Clint said. Either time, he added to himself.

"You mean . . . oh well, then I'm definitely gonna bet," Short said.

"What do you mean?"

"That's how she fought even though she'd had sex last night?" Short asked.

"Yeah, but she only went— what? Five rounds? What if she has to go longer?"

"Okay, so lay off tonight," Short said. "If you have to have a woman, pick out a saloon girl. Leave this girl alone."

Clint almost choked on his beer and said, "*Me* leave *her* alone?"

They had lunch at Chuck's. Clint was warmly greeted by the same waitress, who showed them to a back table.

They ordered the special steak and she went off to get their food and beers.

"She likes you," Short said.

"So?"

"So leave the boxer alone and take the waitress tonight."

"You're assuming a lot."

"No I ain't," Short said. "I know you, Clint."

"Never mind," Clint said. "You just make your bet with the information you have."

"I will, don't worry."

The waitress came with their meals and they suspended their conversation while she laid the plates and beer in front of them.

"Thank you," Clint said.

"Let me know if you need anything else."

As she walked away, Short cut off a hunk of steak and stuck it in his mouth.

"Wow," he said. "You were right."

Clint was glad his first steak had not been a fluke.

"I played some poker last night," Short said.

"With Jack?"

"And some feller named Vince Miles."

"Any good?"

"Fair," Short said, "like Jack."

"So you won."

"Of course," Short said, "but I noticed somethin' odd."

"What's that?"

"In the middle of the game, Miles excused himself and went to the bar for a beer."

"What's unusual about that?"

"Two things," Short said. "One, any of the girls could have got him a beer."

"And two?"

"While at the bar he had a conversation with another man."

"And?"

"And they did everything they could to pretend they weren't talkin' to each other."

"I wonder why they did that?" Clint said. "Did you know the other man?"

"Never saw him before."

"That is odd."

"Just thought you'd like to know," Short said, "since security is your job."

"Right."

"Like keepin' that girl secure tonight," Short said.

"Just keep eating," Clint said.

TWENTY-TWO

After lunch, Clint decided to walk down by the river and see what was going on. They were in the middle of a wrestling match and it just so happened to be the Mauler, the man Brenda was scheduled to box the next day.

Clint watched as Mauler easily dispatched an even larger man with a few fine wrestling moves, as well as brute force. He didn't seem winded when they were done. If he had seemed tired Clint would have felt a little better about Brenda boxing him, since she'd be well rested.

As it stood, the man smiled and waved at the crowd, which was obviously pleased with him. Clint figured the odds on Brenda—no matter what she had done that morning—would be high.

He went to find somebody to place a bet with.

There were several men in the crowd taking bets. After placing his bet, Clint was reminded that Joe Nicholas owed him some money. A small amount, but still, a wager is a wager.

He walked around the ring and found Nicholas talking to the Mauler.

"Clint!" Nicholas said, as if caught doing something he shouldn't be doing. The Mauler nodded at Clint and walked away.

"You owe me some money, Nicky," Clint said.

"What? I thought we were gonna work together on this—" Nicholas started.

"The festival is yours, Nicky," Clint said. "I don't want any part of it. All I want is what I won." He put his hand out.

"Oh, all right. What was it, fifty?"

"A hundred."

Nicholas took out a hundred dollars and handed it to Clint.

"How have the boys been doing for you?" Clint asked.

"Three pickpockets just this morning, and they broke up two fights."

"And your boys?"

"Beck and Hines?" Nicholas said. "I found them in a saloon last night, dead drunk on the money I advanced them."

Clint decided not to comment on Nicholas's choices for security. "I'm going to look around," he said. "What's next?"

"The sharpshooter will be on in an hour. And we've got one more wrestling match."

"Where's the sharp-shoot going to be?"

"At the base of First Street."

"I want to see that," Clint said. "I'll be there."

"Okay." Nicholas turned his attention back to the ring.

Clint worked the crowd for a while. Nicholas had made sure there were booths set up for people to play games, mostly families busting water balloons or spinning a wheel of fortune.

He caught two pickpockets in an hour, both adults, and threatened what he'd do to them if he ever saw them again.

He caught sight of a boy he thought he knew, then realized it was the pickpocket Billy Jensen had caught and taken money off of.

Clint approached the boy, who was standing in front of a booth that was selling cookies and cakes.

When Clint came up, the boy's eyes widened and he started to run, but Clint caught him by the shoulder.

"I wasn't doin' nothin'!" the boy yelled.

"I know you weren't," Clint said. "Relax."

The boy shoved his hands in his pockets.

"What are you doing here?"

"I was just lookin' at the cakes," he said. "I wanted to bring some home to my ma and my sisters."

"Why don't you?"

"Because you took my money away."

"Oh yeah, that's right, we did." Clint put his hand in his pocket, came out with the boy's coins, the extra coins that Jensen had tossed in, and whatever coins he had. The money he handed the boy filled both of his small hands.

"What's this?"

"That's your money."

"But—"

"But what?" Clint asked. "Not enough?"

"No, no," the boy said, "it's . . . enough!"

"Now go buy your family some food!" Clint said.

"Geez, mister," the boy said. "Thanks. My ma and sisters are gonna be so happy." The boy ran right up to the booth and started buying cakes.

TWENTY-THREE

When it got dark, Nicholas had a fireworks display going down by the river. People gathered to watch. Perfect place for pickpockets. Clint was working the crowd along with both Billy Jensen and Walt Denver.

Nicholas came up next to him and said, "We got a poker game starting in half an hour."

"Where?"

"Upstairs from the Colorado," Nicholas said. "Talk to the bartender."

"Who's playing?"

"You'll find out when you get there," Nicholas said. "We need to make sure nothing goes wrong there."

"You got a dealer?"

"Yeah."

"How many tables?"

"Just one."

"What's the buy-in?"

"Ten thousand, six players."

Not really big money, Clint thought, but not chicken

feed. It was an amount that might attract some attention.

"I'll go over and have a look around," Clint said. "Meet the dealer, and the players."

"Okay," Nicholas said. "Thanks."

Clint tracked down Jensen and Denver and told them where he'd be.

"Do we take anybody in?" Denver asked.

"No," Clint said. "The sheriff won't be any help. Just keep doing what we've been doing."

"Okay," Jensen said.

"If you need me, come and get me. Also, when the fireworks are over, you can relieve me."

"Okay."

Clint entered the Colorado. The fireworks had done nothing to hinder their business. He went to the bar.

"Beer?" the man asked.

"Upstairs," Clint said. "Nicholas told me to see you?"

"This way."

He took Clint behind the bar and through a curtained doorway to a stairway.

"Up there."

Clint looked up the stairs. It was a narrow walkway, great place for an ambush.

"I'll watch your back," the bartender said. "Those are my instructions."

Clint studied the man. He wasn't armed, but that didn't mean he couldn't step through the curtain and grab the shotgun Clint had seen under the bar.

But if this man were to ambush him, it would mean he'd been set up by Joe Nicholas. He didn't think that was going to happen.

"Okay," he said.

"First door on the right after you go in."

He went up the stairs without looking back. When he went through the door at the top, he found himself in a hallway. He went to the first door on the right, which was open. There were three men in the room, and a green felt poker table with a woman seated at it, shuffling cards and stacking chips.

He looked at the three players. He knew one, Luke Short. He walked over to the lady dealer first.

"Hello."

She looked up at him with no-nonsense eyes. She was in her late thirties, had her hair pulled back, and was wearing a white shirt and black bow tie. No makeup. A handsome woman who would blossom when she dressed up. Or smiled.

"You Adams?"

"That's right."

"This is the setup," she said. "I just opened the deck. I'm gonna put ten grand in chips at each place."

"Okay," Clint said. "I'm going to talk to these three players. You know them?"

"No," she said. "I don't know any of the players personally. That's why I'm here."

"Good."

Clint walked over to the three players.

"Luke."

"Clint. Meet Eric Drake and Hank Stuart. Fellas, this is Clint Adams."

"Are you playing, Mr. Adams?" Stuart asked. He was a middle-aged man dressed like a gambler, but that didn't keep him from looking like a politician. He wore wire-framed glasses that he squinted over, for some reason.

"No," Clint said, "I'm handling security."

"Well, that should make us feel safe," Drake said. He

was younger, tall, well built with broad shoulders that filled out his jacket like a dock worker, but he had the hands of a gambler: smooth and well taken care of.

"Who are the other three players?" Clint asked, looking at Short.

"Well, Jack and that fella Miles I told you about . . . and we don't know who the sixth player is."

"Well then," Clint said, "we'll all just be surprised together."

TWENTY-FOUR

Three-Fingered Jack came in next, putting his hand out to shake Clint's.

"Nice to see you," he said. "Too bad you're not playin'."

"I think you have your hands pretty full with Luke at the table," Clint said.

The next man in was Vince Miles. Clint studied him intently. Miles looked back at him with relaxed eyes, so if he was up to something, he was very good at hiding it.

"It's a pleasure to meet you," Miles said, shaking Clint's hand. "Anyone know who the sixth man is?"

"Not a clue," Jack said. "Should be interestin', though. It's somebody who can afford the ten thousand dollars."

"He's still got fifteen minutes," Short said. "Why don't we grab our seats." He went to the table.

"Are we assigned seats?" he asked the dealer.

"Sit wherever you like," she said.

"I'll be right back," Clint said. "I'm going to check the hall, and the rest of this floor."

There were three other rooms on the floor, all like the

one he'd just left, no windows. And there was no other stairway. He went back to the room, found the five men seated,
still waiting for the sixth.

He waited, too.

Rusty Cooper sidled up next to Nicholas and both men
watched the fireworks.

"You gonna talk to the mayor again tomorrow?" he asked.

"Oh yeah," Nicholas said. "I've got somethin' new to offer him."

"The girl?"

"That's right."

"You think she can win another fight?"

"Damn, I hope so," Nicholas said. "Did you see her?"

"I did."

"What'd you think?"

"I wouldn't want to get in the ring with her," Cooper
said, "but what will happen when she gets in with the
Mauler?"

"I guess we'll have to wait and see."

When the sixth man arrived, it was no surprise to anyone.

No one seemed to know who he was, but the only way
he could have gotten up the stairs was if he was, indeed, the
sixth player.

"Mike McCloud," he said to the room. "Sorry if I'm
late."

"You're just in time," Short said. "The game's about to
start."

McCloud sat down, and the dealer began to deal.

Clint took up position across the room. From there he
could see the door and the entire table. Every so often he'd
take a walk around the table. If anybody was cheating, he

would have known it. Everything seemed to be on the up-and-up, and Luke Short started off by winning the first three hands.

It didn't take long to realize that three of the men at the table were not professional players; they simply had the money to buy in.

The money was going to go back and forth between Luke Short, Three-Fingered Jack, and maybe Vince Miles, unless one of the other three got lucky.

Clint enjoyed watching the dealer work. She was very efficient, keeping track of the pot and the players. She was a very good table general.

He wondered what her name was. He should have asked.

When the fireworks finished, Billy Jensen and Walt Denver walked to the Colorado Saloon. They presented themselves to the bartender, and he sent them upstairs.

When they entered the room, Clint was making a slow circuit around the table. He joined them at the door.

"I'm going to get some sleep," he said. "You younger fellas can catch the game."

"Both of us?"

"Split the time up any way you want," Clint said. "I'll be in my room at the Bullhead."

"Okay with you if one of us stays up here and one downstairs?"

"I don't care," Clint said. "Just don't get drunk."

"We won't," Denver said.

Jensen shook his head.

TWENTY-FIVE

When Clint got back to his room, he found Brenda sleeping in his bed. She was curled up under the sheet, obviously naked, fast asleep. He backed out of the room right away, not wanting to wake her. He decided to go down to the saloon for a while.

The Bullhead Saloon only had a few men in it, all seated at tables, nodding over their beers. Clint went to the bar, ordered a beer.

"Losing your business to the Colorado?" Clint asked the bartender.

"No," the bartender said. "This is the way it usually is. We can't compete with the Colorado."

"Oh."

"Plus the festival," the barman said.

At that moment, the batwing doors opened and Clint was surprised to see the sheriff walk in.

"Sheriff," the bartender said.

"Jay. Beer."

The lawman turned to Clint.

"Adams. Why aren't you at the Colorado? That's where all the action is."

"That's why I'm over here."

"Yeah," Abernathy said, accepting his beer from the bartender, "Me, too." He took a healthy swig. "Heard there was some excitement down by the river today."

"Fireworks?"

"No, I meant the boxing."

"Oh, that," Clint said.

"That girl's pretty good, huh?"

"Yeah," Clint said, "she pretty much gave that guy a boxing lesson."

"Must be some money to be made there, huh?" Abernathy asked.

"You a betting man, Sheriff?"

"On occasion," Abernathy said, "if the odds are right."

"Well, I'll bet the odds will be pretty good tomorrow. Her next opponent is supposed to be pretty good."

"You bettin'?" Abernathy asked.

"You hunt me down tonight to ask me if you should bet, Sheriff?"

The lawman shrugged. "Maybe just lookin' for a little inside information," he admitted.

"Is that legal, Sheriff?"

"Sure it is."

"What makes you think I know anything?"

"You're the Gunsmith."

Clint waited for more, then said, "What does that prove? Just because I can shoot a gun doesn't mean I know anything about anything."

"You play poker. You're a gambler, not just a gunman," Abernathy said.

"You know a lot about me."

"I'm supposed to know," the man said. "I'm the law. Plus, you've been seen with her."

Clint drank his beer, waved at the barman for another. "And bring one more for the sheriff."

"Thanks," Abernathy said. "So, whaddaya say?"

"About what?"

"Should I bet on her tomorrow or not?"

Clint acted like he was mulling it over, then said, "Sure, why not?"

The sheriff accepted his second beer from the bartender. "Here's to ya," he said.

The sheriff left and Clint stayed to have two more beers before he went back to his room. Maybe he could get into bed next to Brenda without waking her.

He entered the room quietly, removed his clothes, and moved to the bed. She was lying mostly on the left side, so he lifted the sheet to get in, but stopped short to look at her naked butt. He was wearing only underwear, and his cock started to thicken.

Damn. He stopped looking and got into bed next to her. The heat beneath the sheet from her body was intense. He rolled onto his back and tried to ignore it. No luck. His cock was fully hard now.

He thought about what Luke Short had told him about sex and boxing. He'd heard it before, but never believed it. Maybe it was different for women, though. Maybe she needed to have sex so that she'd fight the way she did that morning.

"You gonna do somethin', or what?" she asked.

"Only," he said, "because I've been telling people to bet

on you, and I think you fight better when you have sex."

"Whatever you have to tell yourself," she said, reaching behind her and palming his cock. "Just come on! I gotta get back to sleep."

TWENTY-SIX

Clint moved up close to Brenda, letting his cock lie against the cleft between her ass cheeks. She moaned, pressing her butt harder against him. Then she moved her legs so he could slide up between her thighs and inside of her wet pussy.

"I've never seen a woman get as wet, so fast, as you do," he said.

"And I'll bet you've seen lots of women, huh?" she asked, closing her eyes as he began to move in and out of her.

He reached around to rub her breasts while he fucked her, then moved his hand down between her thighs, rubbing her there.

"Oh my God!" she said and began to buck against him. Gasping, she said, "Nobody's ever hit my trigger as quick as you do!"

In her ear he said, "That must be why they call me the Gunsmith?"

She laughed, moved away from him so he slid out of

her. She slithered down between his legs, tossing the sheet off, and pressed her face to his hot column of flesh. She licked him up and down before taking the swollen tip into her mouth and wetting it with her tongue. Then she took him deeper and her head began to bob up and down on him.

"Jesus, you're a talented girl," he gasped.

"That's me," she said, releasing him for a moment, "boxer . . . and whore!"

She took him back into her mouth and lovingly suckled him. She wrapped one hand around the base of his cock, then cupped his testicles with the other one and continued to suck him until he was straining to keep from shouting as he came and came . . .

They fell asleep with arms and legs entwined, awoke the same way.

"Breakfast?" he asked.

"Is that what you're callin' it today?" she asked.

"No," he said, "I mean a real breakfast."

"Oh yeah," she said. "I'm starvin'."

They got up and dressed, went down to the hotel dining room. He ordered steak and eggs for both of them and plenty of coffee.

"Don't you want to get your own room?" he asked her.

"Why?" she asked. "Don't you like the arrangement?"

"I'm thinking you'll get more rest with your own room," he said. "And since you've made me your manager, I'm willing to get you one."

She thought about it, then said, "Why not? How about some new clothes, while we're at it?"

"I tell you what," he said. "After breakfast, we'll get you a room. You win tonight, I'll buy you some new clothes."

"You got a deal."

"Luke Short is going to bet on you with everything he won yesterday," Clint said.

"That much?"

"I know," Clint said. "It's a heavy burden. The sheriff is also going to bet on you."

"And how about you?"

"Oh yeah," he said, "me, too."

"All you've got?"

"Oh no," he said. "I've seen the Mauler at work. But I'll make a sizable bet. That is, if you tell me you can win."

"Of course I can win," she said. "In fact, I will win."

"You're that confident?"

"I've seen the Mauler in action, too," she said. "He's slow. That means he's perfect for me."

"Where did you learn to be so confident?" he asked.

"Same place I learned to be so good," she said.

The waiter came with their platters and set them down. Clint poured two more cups of coffee.

"I just thought of something," he said.

"What's that?" she asked around a mouthful of steak and eggs.

"Are you betting on yourself?"

She smiled. "With what? I don't have any money."

"Then why are you doing this?" he asked.

"To prove a point," she said. "That not only can I compete with men, I can beat them. The money will come later."

"If you get together with Joe Nicholas, you can probably make some money now."

She made a face and said, "He's not my type. I wouldn't trust him."

"Can't say I blame you on that count," he said.

"Why don't you just keep bettin'," she said, "keep bein' my manager, and keep takin' care of me . . . for now."

TWENTY-SEVEN

After they finished their breakfast, Clint and Brenda went to the front desk and got her a room.

"Not as nice as yours," she said when they got upstairs, "but it'll do."

"Good," he said. "Use it to get some rest. There's going to be a lot of money riding on you tonight."

"I'll have to go to your room to get my gloves and gear."

"Go ahead," he said, handing her the key. "Lock it when you're done and leave the key at the desk."

"Where are you off to?" she asked.

"I'm going to find Luke Short, and tell him to make his bet."

"And make yours?"

"Yes."

"Don't worry," she said. "Your key—and your money—are safe with me."

"Glad to hear it," he said.

* * *

Clint found Luke Short having breakfast at Chuck's Steak-house. The waitress greeted him warmly, showed him to Short's table, and brought him some coffee.

"What's goin' on?" Short asked.

"You doing okay in the poker game?" Clint asked.

"I'm doin' fine," he said. "We lost a player already. Put too much faith in two pair."

"Who was it?"

Short shrugged. "He's gone. Who remembers?"

"So not Jack, and not Vince Miles?"

"No."

"How are they doing?"

"Comin' in just behind me. I was hoping for a little more competition."

"Should be easy money, then."

"You know me," Short said. "It's not about the money."

"Yeah, right."

Short smiled. "Well, not always. What's goin' on with you? How's your girl?"

"She says she's going to win."

"Does she know who she's fightin'?"

"Yes," Clint said. "She says he's big but slow. Tailor-made for her."

"Who is this girl?" Short asked.

"Right now we have to take her at face value," Clint said. "She's a woman who can fight men, and beat them at their own game."

"If she wins tonight, the odds won't be so good tomorrow."

"I guess that depends again on who she fights."

"I'll have to bet big."

"Not all?"

"I'll keep just enough," Short said. "What about you?"

"I'll bet just enough," Clint said.

"And there's the difference between us."

"You're a gambler before anything else, Luke," Clint said. "I'm not."

"What are you more than anythin' else, Clint?" Short asked.

"That's something I'm still trying to figure out," Clint said without hesitation.

"Lemme know when you figure it out."

They walked out of Chuck's together.

"It's too quiet in this town," Short said.

"With all the fireworks that were going off last night?" Clint asked.

"You know what I mean," Short said. "With this many people in town for a festival, there should be some fightin' going on. Some shots fired."

"I know," Clint said.

He looked at the street. It looked like Nicholas was getting his wish: There seemed to be more people in town than the day before. He'd be able to tell better when he got down to the river.

"Where you headed?" Short asked.

"The river."

"I'll come along," Short said. "I got a feelin' it's not gonna stay quiet forever."

They started walking.

"How'd my boys do last night?"

"Stayed alert, relieved each other."

"Sober?"

Short shrugged. "Relatively."

"All I can ask, I guess," Clint said.

TWENTY-EIGHT

Rusty Cooper opened the door to his hotel room in response to a knock. Standing in the hall were Cal Barnes and Harry Fields.

"Come on in before somebody sees ya," Cooper said.

They entered quickly and he closed the door behind them.

"Anybody follow you?" Cooper asked.

"No," Fields said, "why would anybody follow us?"

"I just wanna be sure," Cooper said.

"Nobody's been payin' any attention to us," Barnes said. "What's goin' on?"

"You boys up for a little job?" Cooper asked.

"What kinda job?" Fields asked.

"The kind that could make you a lot of money," Cooper said.

"How much money?"

"The kind of money that can change your life."

"Who do we have to kill?" Fields asked.

"Have you boys heard of the Gunsmith?"

Barnes and Fields exchanged a glance . . .

Cooper sat and listened to Fields and Barnes tell their tale of trying to kill Clint Adams.

"So that's it," Barnes said.

"And he never saw you?"

"Never," Fields said.

"He even came into the saloon where we were sittin' right by the door," Barnes said. "He never gave us a second look."

"Or a first one," Fields added.

Cooper knew that was wrong. A man like Clint Adams looked at everybody in the room when he entered, but if he didn't recognize them, that was fine.

"So, are we in?" Barnes asked.

"Aren't you interested in what you'll have to do?" Cooper asked.

"For the kind of money you're talkin' about," Barnes said, "it don't really matter."

Fields nodded his agreement.

"Okay," Cooper said, "it won't be 'til the end of the week, but here's what we're gonna do . . ."

Clint and Short got to the river in time for another wrestling match. They didn't stay to watch, though, because they were interested in seeing the trick shooter.

"What's this fella's name?" Short asked. "This—what is he? A sharpshooter? Or trick shooter?"

"I think he's both," Clint said, "and I don't know his name, but he's supposed to have a tent somewhere along here."

When they found it, they saw that he not only had a tent,

but a stage built in front of it. A crowd of people had gathered in front to watch the tricks.

As Clint and Luke Short joined the crowd at the back, a flap opened and a man stepped from the tent. He was wearing what, for some reason, most trick shooters—even Annie Oakley—think of as their uniform—buckskins.

Joe Nicholas also appeared on the stage.

"Ladies and gentlemen," he shouted. "Allow me to present the greatest trick shooter in all the world—Wild Bill Flanagan."

"Wild Bill Flanagan?" Luke Short said to Clint. "Jesus."

"He better be good to live up to the Wild Bill name," Clint said. He'd known two Wild Bills in his life—Hickok and Longley—and he doubted that this man could be as good as either one of those.

Out of the corner of his eye, Clint saw that Billy Jensen had also come to watch the exhibition—and watch the crowd. He assumed Walt Denver was watching the spectators by the wrestling ring.

Wild Bill started with clay targets. He had an assistant, a pretty girl dressed in black stockings and a sparkly red dress. She had a red ribbon tied in her raven black hair.

She stood at one end of the stage while he stood at the other, and he shot clay targets out of her hands and her mouth. In each case, he made a show out of aiming one of the silver pistols he wore on his hips in a double rig. He didn't miss once.

After the clay targets, he had his assistant—he introduced her as Julie—bring out a deck of cards. Wild Bill proceeded to drill all the aces right through the center.

When he was finished with the cards, he and his assistant bowed to some scattered applause, and then she stepped to the front.

"Would anyone from the audience like to come up and hold a card, or a clay target, in your hand? Or perhaps your mouth?"

"Why don't you have Clint Adams come up there?" somebody shouted.

Clint and Short looked around to see who had spoken, but they couldn't spot the person. Clint knew it wasn't Joe Nicholas, although he wouldn't have put it past him.

"Yeah, shoot against the Gunsmith!" somebody else called.

Julie turned to look at Wild Bill, who nodded to her.

"If the Gunsmith is really in the audience, we'd be happy to have him come up and shoot against us."

TWENTY-NINE

"You gonna do it?" Short asked.

"No," Clint said. "I'm not here to perform."

"There he is," somebody said. "Right over there."

The crowd turned to look, and then the people in front of him and Luke Short parted, so that he had a path to the stage—if he wanted it.

Flanagan stepped forward, put his hand on Julie's shoulder. She stepped back a few steps.

"What about it, Mr. Adams?" the trick shooter asked. "Would you be interested in a little shooting match?"

"No," Clint said. "That's not why I'm here. You're the performer."

"But I think the folks here would really enjoy a little competition."

Clint studied the man on the stage. He appeared to be in his mid-thirties—young enough to be cocky, old enough to know better.

Joe Nicholas was standing in front of the stage, and he turned to look hopefully at Clint, to see if he'd be willing to shoot. But before Clint could respond again, Nicholas jumped up on stage.

"Now wait a minute," he called out. "If Flanagan and Adams are gonna have a shoot-off, it won't be done here today, and it won't be free. It'll be a special event of the festival."

"It's not going to be an event at all," Clint called out. "That's not what I was brought here for."

"Ah, he's scared," somebody said.

"Yeah, he's yellah."

"No he ain't," a third voice yelled. "He ain't got nothin' to prove."

"Folks, folks," Nicholas said, "the trick shooting exhibition is over for this afternoon. Move over to the ring area for more wrestling and boxing."

As the crowd began to disperse, Flanagan went back into his tent with his assistant. Joe Nicholas came running over to Clint.

"Clint," he said, "I'll pay you! Do you know how many tickets we'll sell?"

"You're forgetting one thing," Luke Short said.

"What's that?" Nicholas asked.

"People would want their money back when it was over," Short said.

"Whaddaya mean? Why?"

"Because it wouldn't be any competition," Short said. "That man can't shoot with Clint."

"Whaddaya mean? You saw him shoot those targets! Out of the girl's mouth!"

"Doesn't matter," Short explained. "There was no pressure."

"What do you mean, no pressure? He coulda killed the girl."

"There was nobody shooting with him," Short said. "No competition. Under pressure, this man would falter. He'd never stand up to the pressure."

Nicholas looked at Clint.

"Is he right?"

"It doesn't matter, Nicky," Clint said. "I'm not doing it." With that, he turned and walked away.

Nicholas looked at Short. "Why won't he do it?"

"Clint doesn't perform on cue, Joe," Short said. "And I can't say I blame him."

He started to walk away, but Nicholas stopped him. "Luke, you could talk him into it."

"What makes you think so?"

"You're his friend," Nicholas said, "he respects you. Come on, Luke, I'll cut you in."

"For what?"

"A piece of the action," Nicholas said. "People will pay to see the Gunsmith outshoot that kid."

"Or get outshot," Short said.

"You really think that could happen?"

"No."

He started away again. Nicholas grabbed his arm, but when Short—the smaller man—gave Nicholas a hard look, he let go.

"Come on, Luke . . ."

"Forget it," Short said. "It's not up to me to make him do something he don't wanna do."

"Luke—"

"I've got to go play poker, Joe," Short said.

"Yeah," Nicholas said, "okay . . ."

Short walked away, headed back to the saloon while Joe Nicholas walked over to the ring.

THIRTY

Clint grabbed Billy Jensen after the exhibition and said, "Make sure you watch the wrestling and boxing crowds. You and Walt."

"Where will you be?"

"Right now I'm going over to the Colorado," Clint said. "After that probably the Bullhead. Then I'll be back here."

"Okay."

Clint left and walked to the Colorado. He was standing at the bar with a beer in his hand when Luke Short walked in.

"Beer?" Clint asked.

"One before I go upstairs."

Clint waved to the bartender.

"Nicholas try to talk you into talking me into shooting?" he asked.

"Oh, yeah."

"What'd you say?"

"I said no."

"That's all?"

"I said it wasn't my place to talk you into something you didn't want to do."

Short accepted the beer from the bartender.

"That kid can shoot," Short said.

"At targets," Clint said. "And he's no kid. He should change his name."

"You mean the Wild Bill?"

Clint nodded.

"I thought that might bother you."

Clint didn't comment.

"Is that why you don't want to shoot?"

Clint hesitated, then said, "Maybe part of it."

"What's the other part?"

"The other part is what I said," Clint answered. "I don't perform. Especially when it's not what I agreed to do."

"Why *did* you agree to this?" Short asked.

"To tell you the truth, I don't know," Clint said. "I have to stop agreeing to things, though. After the last few times, I'm starting to feel used."

"Like what?"

Clint told Short about the business he went through with a friend who had a new Mississippi riverboat.

"And he still hasn't turned up," he ended.

"Probably at the bottom of the river."

"Probably so."

"Well, he tried to use you," Short said. "He deserved it."

"I don't know that he deserved to die."

"So now Nicholas is usin' you."

"Or trying to."

Short finished his beer. "I'm going up," he said. "Gonna be a long day."

"Good luck."

Short went behind the bar to go through the doorway to the stairs, but stopped and turned back.

"I just want to tell you one thing."

"What's that?"

"This whole thing," he said, "doesn't feel right to me."

"How so?"

"I don't know," Short said, "it just . . . feels wrong. Be careful."

Short waved and went up the stairs to the second floor.

Clint stood at the bar and had a second beer. Luke Short was a man with good instincts. If something felt bad to him, then it was bad.

Joe Nicholas's festival was a flop, as far as Clint could see. And it seemed as if he should have known that. The location was bad. So the question was, why did he choose to have the event in Bullhead City?

Clint left the saloon and walked to the sheriff's office.

He ran into the sheriff on the way to the man's office.

"Where are you headed?" Abernathy asked.

"To see you, actually."

"Well, I'm on my way to the office. Come on."

They walked to the office together.

"Still not many people in town for the festival," the lawman said. "You notice that?"

"I noticed."

"But your friend Nicholas, and the mayor, they seem excited about this lady boxer."

"Yeah, she seems to be pretty good."

"Well, they think they're gonna make some money off of her."

"They might."

"Her first fight wasn't a fluke?"

"I guess we'll find that out tonight when she fights again."

"Well," the sheriff said, "I got my bet down on your word."

"All I know is, she's confident."

When they got to the office, the sheriff opened the door and said, "So, what's on your mind?"

THIRTY-ONE

"You think there's somethin' goin' on in town?" the lawman asked.

"I just think this whole festival thing is . . . wrong," Clint said.

"So you're with me on this festival, now?" Abernathy asked. "It shouldn't be happenin'?"

"I don't know that it shouldn't be," Clint said, "I'm just thinking there might be something else going on here."

"Like what?"

"That's what I'm asking you."

"I don't know of anythin'," Abernathy said, "but that don't mean there ain't somethin'. Me and the mayor don't see eye to eye. I think this is gonna be my last term as sheriff, so there could be somethin' goin' on that I don't know about."

"So how do we find out?"

The sheriff shrugged.

"I guess you'll have to ask the mayor."

"Can you get me in to see him?"

"No problem," Abernathy said. "I walk in on the old bastard all the time. Come on."

Clint followed Abernathy to City Hall. He remembered how he had seen Joe Nicholas coming out the front door. Obviously Nicholas and the mayor had to work together on this festival.

"Before we go in," Clint said, "tell me about the mayor."

"Whaddaya wanna know?"

"What kind of man is he?"

"He ain't a man," the sheriff said. "He's a politician. He's been mayor here for a long, long time. Too long."

"Is he ready to move on?" Clint asked. "Maybe a higher office?"

"Hell, no," Abernathy said. "He's beyond that. No, he's stuck here as mayor until he dies, I think."

"Why doesn't he just quit?"

"You don't get it. He's a politician. He can't move up, so he's stuck here. He won't give up the office. It's all he's got."

"Family?"

"His wife died, and they never had any kids."

Clint didn't like the sound of that. This sounded to him like a desperate man who would do anything.

"Sounds like I better meet this man."

"Let's go."

The sheriff did exactly what he said he did: When they reached the door to the mayor's office, he barged right in.

"What the hell—" the man behind the desk sputtered. "What have I told you about this, Sheriff?"

"I have someone here who is anxious to meet you, Mayor," Abernathy said. "And he couldn't wait."

The mayor, a florid-faced man in his sixties who carried at least forty pounds too much, all in his belly, stood and stared at Clint.

"So?" he demanded. "Who is he?"

"Mayor Soames, this is Clint Adams," the sheriff said, "the Gunsmith."

The mayor reacted as if he thought Clint was there to kill him. He shrank back and raised his hands defensively, which Clint found odd.

"What's wrong?" he demanded. "Why are you acting this way?"

"Well . . . you're a killer, aren't you?" Soames asked.

"No more than you are, Mayor," Clint said. "I don't kill for no reason." Clint moved closer to the desk. The mayor shrank back farther until he bumped into the window.

"Unless you know of a reason I should kill you?" Clint Asked.

"Uh, no . . ."

"Does someone have a reason to have you killed?" Clint asked. "And you're thinking they hired me?"

"I, uh, no . . ."

"Then I suggest you sit down, Mayor, before you fall down," Clint said. "I'm only here to talk to you."

"Talk?" the mayor asked. "About what?"

"About this damn festival," the sheriff said, "which I told you was a mistake in the first place. The Gunsmith agrees."

"I . . . I see," the mayor said. Warily, he sat back down in his chair. He took out a handkerchief and blotted his sweating face.

"Well," he said, "maybe we should talk about it, then."

THIRTY-TWO

"It seems fairly obvious to me, and to the sheriff here, that this festival never should have taken place in this town," Clint said. "There's just not enough population to support it."

"Well . . . we expected people to come from other towns," the mayor said.

"Why would you expect that?" Clint asked. "A festival in Bullhead City? What would the appeal be to make people travel here? How did you get the word out?"

"I—I wasn't involved with that," the mayor said. "That was Joe Nicholas's job."

"Well, it doesn't seem like he did a very good job."

"He got you to come."

"To work security," Clint said, "which obviously wasn't necessary. All we've done is catch a few pickpockets, and most of those were kids. No, something else is going on here."

"Like what?"

"That's why I'm, here," Clint said impatiently. "Is there some kind of payroll in your bank?"

"No, we have a small bank," the mayor said. "There's no payroll in there."

"Is there a stage coming in that's carrying something valuable?" Clint asked.

"No stage."

"Well, your bank could still be hit," Clint said. "I mean, for its regular deposits."

"There ain't much money in there," the sheriff said.

"Your money is in there, isn't it, Mayor?" Clint asked.

"Uh, no," the mayor admitted. "I don't put my money in the bank."

Clint decided not to ask the man where he did keep his money. It was either in his home, or here in his office.

"So you're saying you really thought this festival was going to be successful, and good for the town?"

"Your friend Nicholas convinced me of that!" the mayor complained. "I don't see the hordes of people he said would be coming to town."

"No," Clint said, "I don't, either."

"But now he says you have a new attraction," the mayor said. "Some woman who's boxing with men? And beating them? Is that true?"

"She's fought once and won, yes," Clint said, "but I don't see how she's going to draw people on her own."

"I knew I shouldn't have listened to him," the mayor said. "I had a feeling . . ."

"You should have gone with your feeling, Mayor," Clint said, standing up. He left the office, followed by the sheriff.

When they were outside, Clint asked, "Is he lying?"

"I don't think so."

Clint looked at Abernathy. "Are you lying?"

"No," the lawman said without getting offended.

"Then what's going on?"

"Maybe," the sheriff said, "it's just a failed festival."

"Well, it's definitely that," Clint replied. "But usually Joe Nicholas is too smart to get involved in something that's obviously destined to fail."

"Then I guess you're gonna have to ask him, ain'tcha?" Abernathy said.

"I guess I am."

THIRTY-THREE

Clint wasn't sure what to do next.

The festival was going to run the rest of the week. There'd be wrestling matches, boxing matches, and trick shooting demonstrations most of those days. If the crowd picked up by the last two days, could the festival be called a success? Clint didn't think so. It'd take more than two days to save this thing.

Luke Short was very happy playing in his poker game. He may not have been getting the type of competition he was used to, but at least he'd be cleaning up, which would suit him.

Brenda would be happy to keep fighting and winning, but even if she beat the Mauler later on that night, could she continue to fight men for days and win?

Clint decided to head down to the river and see if he could locate Joe Nicholas. The sheriff was absolutely right: Nicholas was the one who should have the answers to his questions.

*   *   *

Rusty Cooper saw Clint Adams walking down the street toward him and ducked into the hardware store. As Clint walked by, Cooper watched him through the window. Satisfied that Clint had gone by, he stepped out again. Clint Adams wouldn't know him if he saw him; nevertheless, Cooper didn't want to be seen. He turned and continued up the street.

When he got to the Colorado Saloon, he went inside and stepped up to the bar.

"Beer," he said.

"Comin' up," the barman said, and placed one in front of him.

He nursed that beer for twenty minutes until Vince Miles came downstairs.

"Beer," Miles said to the bartender.

"How's the game goin'?" the bartender asked, handing him his beer.

"It's fine," Miles said dismissively.

The bartender took the hint and walked away to wipe some glasses.

With so few people in the saloon, there was no point in the two men pretending not to talk.

"You get two men?" Miles asked.

"Yeah," Cooper said.

"You know them?"

"I know their type," Cooper said.

"We can get rid of them after?"

"Easily."

"Okay."

"Are you sure about this?" Cooper asked.

"You've asked me that before," Miles said. "I'm positive."

"And they'll be here at the end of the week?" Cooper asked.

"Yes."

"Can you last that long?"

"I can, but it doesn't matter," Miles said. "Even if I lose, I'll just stay around for the rest of the festival. Nobody'll get suspicious."

"There ain't that many people here," Cooper said.

"That doesn't matter, either," Miles said. "Don't worry about anything."

"Yeah," Cooper said, "easy for you to say."

He pushed away his empty mug, turned, and walked out of the saloon.

Luke Short watched the game for a few minutes after Miles left the game, then excused himself and went downstairs. He stopped when he saw Miles at the bar, talking to another man. It was the same man he'd seen Miles pretending *not* to talk to the other night. He watched as the two conversed, then watched the other man leave. He decided to step out and confront Miles, see how the man reacted.

"Friend of yours?" Short asked.

"Huh?" Miles turned his head and looked at Short. "Who?"

"The man who just left," Short said. He signaled the bartender for a beer.

"Oh, uh, no, I never saw him before," Miles said. "He was askin' directions."

"I see."

"I couldn't help him," Miles said. "I haven't seen much more of the town than my hotel room and this place." He pushed his mug away and said, "I better get back. See you there."

"Sure."

After Miles left, the bartender came over.

"I heard what he said," the bartender said. "If that guy was lookin' for directions, why didn't he ask me?"

"That's a good question," Luke Short said.

THIRTY-FOUR

Clint walked to the river, looked around the ring and the tents, but couldn't locate Joe Nicholas. When he passed the trick shooter's tent, though, the shooter's assistant came out.

"Mr. Adams," she said.

"Julie, right?"

"That's right."

Up close she looked about twenty-two or -three.

"Can I help you with something?" she asked. "Are you looking for someone?"

"Joe Nicholas."

"I'm sorry," she said, "I don't know where he is. Haven't seen him this morning."

"Okay," Clint said, "thanks."

"Could I, uh, talk to you for a moment, Mr. Adams?" she asked.

"Sure."

"Can we walk along the river?"

"Why not?"

They started to walk.

"What's on your mind?"

"What did you think of the show?" she asked.

"You mean, Wild Bill Flanagan?"

She laughed.

"His real name is David," she said, "David Flanagan. He thought 'Wild Bill' would sound better."

"Well," Clint said, "it was already somebody's name."

"I know," she said. "Wild Bill Hickok. That's where he got it."

"Maybe he should have stuck to his own name."

She turned her head and stared at him. "Does that make you angry?" she asked. "That he took that name?"

"As a matter of fact," Clint said, "it does."

"But . . . why?"

"Because Jim Hickok was a friend of mine."

"Jim?" she said. "I thought his name was Bill."

"His name was James Butler Hickok and he was my friend."

"Oh," she said. "Oh, I didn't know."

They walked in silence for a little while.

"I'm sorry," she said. "I had no idea."

"What did you want to talk to me about, Julie?" he asked.

"Well . . . shooting."

"What about it."

"I wanted to see if I could talk you into shooting with him. With David."

"No."

"You haven't heard what I have to say," she complained. "I can be pretty persuasive."

"I'm sure you can be," he said, "just not this time."

"Why not? You can't be afraid."

"Why not?"

"What?"

"Why can't I be afraid?"

"Well . . . you're the Gunsmith."

"That doesn't matter," he said. "I'm still a man. Things scare me."

"So you are afraid to shoot with him?"

"No, I'm not."

"Then why won't you shoot with him?"

"You mean, against him, don't you?" Clint asked. "Why won't I shoot against him?"

"Yes, that's what I mean."

"Well, I have two reasons," Clint said. "First, that's not what I came here to do."

"And what's second?"

"Second is, I don't perform on cue," Clint said. "But your guy, David, he should have a reason, too. One reason."

"Oh? And what would that be?"

She stopped and faced him, her back to the river. Across the river, he saw men standing thigh deep in the water, fishing. It reminded him that he hadn't fished in a long time.

"He'd be embarrassed."

"What? How?"

"If he expected to beat me, he'd be disappointed."

"How do you know?"

"I saw him shoot."

"And?"

"He's very good shooting at a stationary target, with no pressure."

"No pressure? What would happen if he missed and hit me? That's pressure."

"No, that's not pressure," Clint said. "Shooting against another man, that's pressure. And he wouldn't handle it."

"How do you know?" There was a touch of anger there. He was wondering if he'd got to her.

"This is what I do, Julie," he said. "Whether I like it or not, this gun has been my life. I know when a man can shoot and when he can't."

"You don't know," she said. "You don't know David."

"And you do?"

"Yes."

"What makes you think you know him so well?"

"He's my husband."

"Oh, I see."

"No, I don't think you do see," she said. "We need something, and this festival isn't it. But we came anyway, because we need the money. But if you would shoot with him, things could change."

"Julie," I said, "if I shoot against David and beat him, how will that help?"

She hesitated, then said, "If he shoots against you and wins, it would make all the difference in the world."

"And you're willing to take the chance?" he asked.

"Yes."

"Is he willing to take that chance?"

"Yes."

"You've asked him?"

She hesitated, then said, "He's willing."

"Well," Clint said, "I'm not going to do it."

"Would you meet him?"

"When?"

"Now?"

It was his turn to hesitate. "What good would that do?" he asked.

"Maybe meeting you would help him," she said. "If you won't shoot with him, maybe if you just met him . . ."

"Okay," he said, "okay, Julie. I'll meet him."

THIRTY-FIVE

They walked back to the tent. When they got there, Julie said, "Let me go in and tell him you're here."

"Okay."

"Don't leave, okay?"

"I won't."

She nodded and went inside. In a few minutes she came out again and said, "Will you come in?"

"Sure."

She held the flap back for him and he entered. The inside was lit by lamps, and David Flanagan was standing there in his buckskins, his hat off.

"Mr. Adams," he said. "It's an honor." He extended his hand.

Clint shook hands and said, "It's nice to meet you, Mr. Flanagan."

"Please, call me David."

"Not Wild Bill?"

"No," he said, "not Wild Bill. I'm sorry about that. Julie told me—"

"You couldn't have known," Clint said. "And why should you care?"

"I thought I was . . . honoring him, you know? His memory."

"Look, forget it," Clint said. "You don't have to explain."

Flanagan had both his guns on, and they gleamed as if he'd just polished them.

"You always wear those?" Clint asked.

"No," Flanagan said, "I was just practicing." He unstrapped the guns and set them aside. "You always wear yours, though, right?"

"Pretty much."

"You want somethin' to drink?" the younger man asked. "I think we've got some whiskey. We have any whiskey left, honey?"

"I think we do—" she said, starting forward.

"No, that's okay," Clint said. "I really can't stay. I'm supposed to be working this festival, you know."

"It's not much of a festival, is it?" Flanagan asked.

"I'm afraid not," Clint said. "Just hasn't turned out the way Joe Nicholas wanted it to."

"I figured that when we came," Flanagan said, "but we didn't have much choice. We really needed the money."

"So I heard."

"You know," Flanagan said, "it would be a real honor if you'd agree to shoot against me."

"Well, Julie and I talked about that, Mr. Flanagan," Clint said.

"Please, call me Dave."

"I don't know if you'll want to be on a first-name basis with me when I tell you I won't shoot against you, Dave."

"Sure would be helpful to me if you would, sir," Flanagan said.

"Shooting against me and losing isn't going to help you, Dave."

"You never know," Flanagan said. "I might win."

"Well, we're not going to find out, Dave," Clint said. "I told Julie and now I've told you. So I'll be on my way." He turned, nodded to Julie, and left the tent.

He had walked a few feet when Flanagan called out from behind him.

"Mr. Adams!"

He stopped, and turned. Wild Bill Flanagan was standing there with his guns on. "Mr. Adams," he said. "What would happen if I made you shoot with me?"

"And how would you do that, Dave?"

"By callin' you out."

"Now that wouldn't be smart, Dave," Clint said. "You're talking about doing more than just shooting at targets. Have you ever faced a man with a gun before?"

"No, I haven't," Flanagan said. "But there's always a first time. You had your first time."

"Well," Clint said, "I don't want your first time to be your last, Dave. I'm sure Julie doesn't, either."

Flanagan didn't comment, but he started to flex his hands.

"Julie's right inside the tent, Dave. You want her to watch you die?"

"I'm not talking about now, Clint," Flanagan said. "But sometime before the week is out, I think you'll shoot against me."

"Son," Clint said, "you better hope not."

Clint turned his back, fairly certain Flanagan wouldn't shoot him. If the man had never faced another from the front, he'd most likely never shot a man in the back.

"I guess we'll see about that, Mr. Adams," Flanagan said to Clint's back. "I guess we'll just have to see about that."

THIRTY-SIX

Clint spent the rest of the afternoon by the river, watching wrestling, watching what crowd there was— mostly families with kids. There were some game booths set up so that parents could win Kewpie dolls for their kids, or so boys could win them for their girlfriends.

Joe Nicholas finally appeared, came up to Clint, and asked, "Is your girl ready?"

"I don't know," he said. "I haven't seen her today. Where have you been?"

"I've been workin'," Nicholas said. "Sending telegrams, tryin' to bring in more people."

"Any luck?"

"I might have," Nicholas said. "We'll know by tomorrow. Meanwhile, why don't you go and get your girl? You are her manager, right?"

"Right," Clint said. "What about Mauler. Is he ready to go?"

"He says he's gonna tear her apart."

"Does he know he's boxing, not wrestling?" Clint asked.

"I'll remind him," Nicholas said. "Go!"

Clint knocked on Brenda's door, hoping that she'd changed her mind. But when the door opened there she was, dressed for the ring, carrying her gloves with her.

"About time you came to get me," she said. "You are my manager, right?"

"That's right."

"Well, then, let's go," she said. "You can help me get my gloves on."

They left the hotel and started walking toward the river. Along the way, people called out to Brenda—men and women—wishing her luck.

"Wow, word has certainly got around," she said.

"And I don't think it's an accident," Clint said. "Nicholas has been hard at work."

When they got to the ring area, the wrestlers had been cleared out. There were people around the ring. A lot of people. Brenda stopped.

"Where did all these people come from?" she asked.

"I don't know," Clint said, also surprised. "Maybe Nicholas has been working harder than I thought."

They worked their way to Brenda's corner and he helped her on with her gloves. She leaned in and pressed her mouth to his ear.

"If you had come for me earlier," she said, "you could've helped me wrap my breasts."

"Next time invite me," he said.

She smiled and promised, "I will."

With her gloves laced on, she climbed into the ring. Clint hesitated, then got into the ring with her. They stood in their corner, staring across at the Mauler, who had no second with him.

"He thinks he's going to beat you easily," Clint said. "He told Nicholas he'd destroy you. He's got no respect for you. Use that."

"I always do," she said.

Nicholas got in the ring and introduced the combatants. To Clint's surprise, the Mauler was booed when he was introduced.

"The crowd's on your side," Clint said, "but they're still betting on him."

"That's their problem," she said.

"Good luck," he said, and started to get out of the ring.

She stopped him with her gloved hands on his arm and said, "Kiss for luck?"

Without hesitation, he kissed her on the mouth.

She smiled and said, "Thanks," and the bell rang for round one.

THIRTY-SEVEN

Brenda advanced to the center of the ring with her hands up. Mauler, on the other hand, plodded toward his opponent and started swinging right away. His punches were meant to take her head off, but he swung three times and none of the punches connected. Off balance, he turned and caught a left jab on the cheek that opened a cut.

He roared, straightened up, and came at Brenda again, swinging. This time, as she dodged four punches in a row, she also landed four jabs on the same cheek. The cut became uglier each time, until the lower left half of his face was covered with blood. The ring floor was also dotted with it.

The bell rang and the referee had to forcibly push the Mauler back to his corner. Someone outside the ring handed him a towel and he wiped his face with it, but all he did was make things worse.

"You've got him," Clint called up to Brenda. "Keep working on that cheek."

"I can't," she said.

"Why not?"

"I don't want to scar him for life," she said. "I just want to beat him."

"Well then," he said, "you better knock him out."

For the next six rounds she tried, but other than bloodying him, the man seemed to be cut from granite. He absorbed the punches and kept coming. Over the course of the first seven rounds he never laid a glove on her, but it seemed to Clint the punches were getting closer. Still, none had landed.

Until the eighth.

She was jabbing at him, and Clint could see she was trying to avoid the cuts—on both sides of his face now—rather than work on them. To that end, she was jabbing him in the forehead, probably the hardest part of his body.

Suddenly, Clint saw her flinch as her left glove glanced off his forehead. She had hurt her hand on that punch. The pain in her hand momentarily flustered her just as the Mauler threw a murderous right. She avoided most of it, but the blow glanced off her right cheek and knocked her back against the ropes. As the Mauler started to wade in on her the bell rang again, saving her.

She came back to her corner remained standing, as she had all the other rounds, but Clint could see her knees were weak.

He got up on the ring apron so he could shout in her ears, because the crowd was getting louder and louder. From there, he could see the bruise on her cheek.

"You okay?"

"Fine," she said.

"You hurt your hand," he said. "How bad?"

She looked at him. Her eyes were bright and clear. That was a good sign.

"It's bruised," she said, "but not broken."

"Can you throw it?"

"I guess I'll find out."

"Brenda," he said, "two things."

"What?"

"Knock him out!"

"And what's the second one?"

"Don't get hit again!"

Round nine went like most of the others, with the Mauler swinging wildly and not connecting. Brenda was apparently able to throw left jabs, but not as often. She avoided hitting his forehead. Unfortunately, she still didn't want to work on his cuts, which meant she ended up punching him on the shoulders and chest. All that did was make him mad.

Mauler's strength was obviously his stamina. As round nine ended, Clint wondered how good Brenda's was.

As she went out for round ten, Joe Nicholas came up alongside him and asked, "What's she doin', tryin' to make it look good?"

"She's trying to knock him out."

"That's not good news, Clint," Nicholas said.

"She knows what she's doing."

"He's so slow! What's her problem?"

"He's strong."

"Why doesn't she work on those cuts?"

What was he supposed to tell Nicholas? That she didn't have a killer instinct?

"Just watch," Clint said.

Nicholas moved away, shaking his head.

The next few rounds went the same. As she went for the thirteenth, Clint found Luke Short next to him.

"Is she okay?"

"Yes."

"I thought he had her when he tagged her earlier."

"One punch."

"A glancing blow," Short said. "If he hits her solid, she'll go down."

"We'll see," Clint said.

"I hope not," Short said, and faded back into the crowd.

After the fifteenth round, he got on the apron again.

"How are your legs?"

"Okay."

"Look at me."

She did. He thought her eyes were a little glassy.

"You can't go much further, can you?"

"I won't need to," she said.

"Why?"

"I made a big bet that I'd knock him out in the fifteenth."

"You . . . what? You've been varying him all this time?"

"He's strong," she said, "but not that strong."

"Where'd you get the money to bet?"

"I used credit."

"Where did you get credit?"

As the bell rang she said, "I used yours."

THIRTY-EIGHT

As she went to the center of the ring for the fifteenth, she walked into a right hand. It seemed to catch her flush on the jaw and she went down onto her back. The Mauler wanted to go after her, but the referee forced him back, then started to count.

Brenda rolled onto her stomach and pushed herself up to her knees. She looked over at Clint. Her mouth was bloody, but she grinned at him and winked. She got to her feet at the count of eight.

The Mauler advanced on her, an eager look on his bruised and battered face. The cuts seemed to have stopped bleeding, but his face was still red. Clint could see how confident that one punch had made him, because he was coming in wide open.

And Brenda caught him with a right of her own.

Mauler had been coming in a crouch, but the punch straightened him up. She hit him again, three quick jabs that opened all the cuts, and then a hard right cross that made his eyes cross.

He staggered back and the crowd started to roar. At some point during the fight, it had started to get dark and lamps had been lit all around the ring. In the flickering light, Brenda advanced on the Mauler and began to throw punches with deadly intent.

She landed two more lefts—her hand apparently not that sore—before throwing another crushing right, which landed flush on the big man's jaw. That was it. His eyes rolled up in his head and he fell face-first onto the ring floor.

Brenda backed away so the referee could count to ten. The onlookers were yelling, and Clint found himself among them, shouting 'til he was hoarse.

". . . eight . . . nine . . . ten . . ."

The place erupted. Probably those screaming the loudest were the ones who had big bets on Brenda to beat the Mauler.

Joe Nicholas happily jumped into the ring and raised her hand. Clint climbed into the ring and Brenda turned, grabbed him, and kissed him soundly.

They climbed out of the ring together and Clint pressed his mouth to her ear and said, "You scared me to death."

"I had to make it look good."

"You have a bruise on your cheek, and a split lip," he said.

"Part of the game," she said.

"Come on," he said, as the crowd buffeted them. "Let me get you out of here."

He led the way, bulling through the crowd while, in the ring, a beaten and dazed Mauler was just being helped to his feet.

Clint got Brenda back to the hotel. Word had already filtered into town that she had won and people on the street cheered her as they walked. When they got to the hotel, Clint told the desk clerk to get some hot water and bring it to her room.

In her room he told her to sit on the bed, but she was still too keyed up to stay still. So while she stood, he untied her gloves and pulled them off.

"Let me see that hand," he said, grabbing it and probing with his thumbs.

"You've done this before," she said.

"I've been in the ring," he said, "and I've worked with fighters before. I've also refereed, so yeah, I've had some experience."

"Why didn't you tell me before?"

He just shrugged.

"It was because you didn't take me serious, isn't it?"

"Maybe," he said without looking at her.

"That's okay," she said. "I understand."

There was a knock on the door. When he opened it, the desk clerk came in with a basin filled with hot water.

"We keep it hot for anyone who wants a bath," he explained.

"Put it on the dresser."

"Yessir."

As the clerk backed out of the room, he ogled Brenda and said, "Congratulations, ma'am."

"You know what?" she said to him. "Since you keep that water hot, set me up with a bath, will you?"

"Yes, ma'am," the clerk said. "Comin' up."

As he closed the door she abruptly pulled off her shirt, revealing her wrapped torso.

"Help me unwrap, will you?" she asked.

Clint found the point where the wrap started and began to undo it. Round and round and then suddenly, her breasts were bare and in his face. She was sweaty and he found the scent of her heady.

"I should rub this redness out," he said. He began to rub the skin of her sides, and her back, and eventually moved his hands to her breasts. Her nipples grew hard beneath his touch.

"I smell like a goat," she said, but did not back away from his touch.

"It doesn't matter to me," he said. "I like the way you smell."

She reached between his legs and felt him through his trousers.

"Wow, you do, don't you?" she said. "You sure you don't wanna wait until after my bath?"

"This suits me if it suits you," he said.

She grabbed his belt, undid it, and said, "Oh, this suits me."

THIRTY-NINE

Clint lifted her sweaty breasts to his mouth, sucked the salt off her nipples. She rubbed him vigorously, feeling his hard cock through his pants. After he had licked her breasts clean, he set about getting the rest of her clothes off. As he removed her pants, the sharp smell of sex came to him from her crotch.

When she was naked, he pushed her down on the bed so that her legs were hanging over the edge. He knelt down on the floor between her legs and attacked her pussy with his mouth and tongue. He had not been this sexually excited in a long time. His heart was pounding, his cock felt like it wanted to explode.

He licked sweat from her thighs, then ran his tongue the length of her sex-and-sweat-slickened slit. She was sweet and sour together, and he loved it. He rubbed his face between her legs and she gasped and reached down to grab his head.

"Oh god," she said, as he continued to lick her, "Je-zuz!"

Her body began to tremble as he quickly brought her to

climax. She released his head and beat her fists on the mattress as the waves of pleasure ran over and through her, forcing her to bite her lip to keep from screaming. She forgot about her split lip, and suddenly she tasted blood again.

Clint got to his feet and quickly undressed. She knew what was coming, so she scooted up on the mattress to give them both enough room. He got on the bed with her, grabbed her legs, roughly spread them, and drove his stiff cock into her.

Her flesh was cold and clammy from the fight, but her pussy was hot and wet. He slid into her easily and she grunted as he fucked her hard. He bulled his way in and out of her, his heart still pounding. He was concerned with his own pleasure now, holding her ankles tightly, keeping her spread as he took her in hard, quick strokes.

"Oh, yeah," she moaned, "God, yes, harder, come on, give it to me . . ."

He gave it to her, but not because she wanted it. He did it because he couldn't help it. His hips moved faster and faster as he fucked her harder and harder, and thinking about how she looked in the ring only served to excite him even more . . .

He kissed her brutally later, splitting her lips again and tasting her blood. She pushed him down so she could slide down between his legs and suck him. He became hard again immediately as she held him with one hand and sucked him up and down, tasting herself on him, her own sweat, her own pussy juice . . .

Clint's excitement, only slightly abated by having fucked her so long until he exploded painfully inside of her, began to mount again as she bobbed up and down on his hard cock, sucking him wetly and noisily.

She was still strong, even after fifteen rounds, grabbed his legs the way he had grabbed hers and spread him so she could lick his balls, his anus, up and down the length of him, before finally taking him into her mouth again. This time she suckled him until she felt he was ready to finish, then climbed aboard and stuffed him inside her again. She rode him hard, flesh slapping flesh as she came down on him, until he once again erupted inside of her . . .

"Jesus!" she said.

"I know!" he said.

"Wow. I'm usually excited after a fight, but I've never really done anything about it. I'm gonna have to do that more often."

"Well," he said, "you have another fight tomorrow. Of course, you'll have to win first . . ."

"Oh, don't worry," she said, reaching down between his legs and grabbing his cock. "If this is my prize, I'll win, all right."

He rolled over and licked her shoulder, still enjoying the taste of her perspiration.

"God, you are the oddest man, Clint Adams," she said. "I stink!"

"You still smell exciting to me," he said.

"Well, I have to have a bath," she said. "If you wanna wait for me, I'll be right back and I'll be clean."

She got off the bed, started dressing again.

"Hmm," he said, watching her, "a clean Brenda as opposed to a sweaty, slightly battered Brenda."

"If you wait," she said, "I'll show you it'll be worth it."

He heard her stomach growl, then, and said, "Seems like your fight worked up another kind of appetite, too."

"Oh yeah," she said, "I need a steak bad."

"I tell you what," he said. "I'll wait and take the clean Brenda out for a steak dinner. How's that sound?"

"Heavenly," she said, "but afterward we can come right back here, right?"

He smiled and said, "Who am I to refuse the champ?"

FORTY

The back door to the house opened and Rusty Cooper stepped inside.

"Anybody see you?" the mayor asked.

"No."

"Come through, then."

The mayor led Cooper from his kitchen to his living room.

"I got word they'll be here tomorrow," he said to Cooper. "It has to be done then."

"It will."

"You have enough men?"

"I do."

"And the gambler?"

"He's ready."

It did not go unnoticed by Cooper that Mayor Soames did not offer him anything to drink, or even invite him to sit.

"You can't let anyone stop you," Soames said. "Not the sheriff, and not Clint Adams."

"Don't worry," Cooper said.

"I am worried," the mayor said. "This town has been my whole life, and now I'm risking it all."

"But look what you're riskin' it for," Cooper said.

"Adams came to see me," the politician said.

"What did he want?"

"He wanted to know if I knew of anything of value in town, or if any kind of a shipment was coming in."

"So he's guessing."

"It's a damn good guess."

"Don't worry about it," Cooper said. "This is why you called me in, right?"

The mayor looked at him for a long time before he said, "Right."

Cooper found Fields and Barnes at Saloon #8. He got a beer and joined them at a table.

"Tomorrow's the day."

"All right!" Barnes said. "It's about time."

"You boys are gonna have to go on watch," Cooper said. "When you spot 'em, one of you will have to come back and get me."

"Just the three of us are gonna do this?" Fields asked.

"Four," Cooper said.

"Is that enough?" Barnes asked.

"If everyone does what I tell them, yeah," Cooper said, "starting with you two."

"Just tell us what to do," Fields said.

"And when," Barnes said.

"Okay," Cooper said, "listen up . . ."

After meeting with the mayor, and then with Fields and Barnes, Cooper went to the Colorado Saloon. He knew the poker game was still going on upstairs. He also knew there were four players left: Luke Short, Vince Miles, Three-Fingered Jack, and Mike McCloud.

He had a beer and waited to see if Miles would come down. When he got to a second beer and the gambler still didn't appear, he got annoyed, but there was nothing he could do. He could not go upstairs. And he couldn't very well leave a message with the bartender.

Or could he?

He called the man over.

"I got a message for one of the poker players upstairs," he said.

"Sorry," the bartender said, "nobody's allowed up there but the players."

"That's okay," Cooper said. "If I give you the message, can you give it to him?"

"Sure, I don't see why not. Say, ain't you the fella was in here askin' directions the other day?"

"Yeah, directions," Cooper said. "You remember the guy I was talkin' to?"

"Yeah, his name's Miles."

"You tell Mr. Miles that the directions he gave me won't be any good until tomorrow."

"What's that mean?" the bartender asked. "Directions is directions, ain't they?"

"You'd think so, wouldn't you?" Cooper asked. "You just give him the message, okay?"

"Sure, sure."

"And nobody else."

"Who else would I give it to?" the bartender asked. "I hope he don't ask me what it means."

"Don't worry," Cooper said. "He'll know what it means."

FORTY-ONE

Clint and Brenda had steak dinners and then he walked her back to her room.

"Not coming in?" she asked.

"You need to get some rest," he said. The bruise on her cheek had turned black and blue, and her lower lip was swollen. "And I've still got work to do."

"Well, if you finish early, come by," she said. "I'm a light sleeper."

He knew that wasn't true, but he told her he would. He kissed her mouth gently and gave her a shove inside. Then he turned, left the hotel, and headed to the Colorado.

As he approached the saloon, a man came out the batwing doors, turned, and went in the opposite direction. Clint was used to two things—people avoiding him because of his reputation, and people coming after him because of it. He wondered if those two bushwhackers were in town? In fact, that might have been one of them.

He entered the Colorado, found it about half full. As he

got to the bar, the bartender already had a beer on it for him.

"Thanks. Who's the fellow who just left?"

"Beats me," the man said. "He left me a message for one of the poker players."

"Which one?"

"Miles," the barman said. "Vince Miles."

"Anything important?"

The man shrugged and said, "Just somethin' about directions. I ain't supposed to tell anybody else."

"Luke Short been down?" Clint asked, changing the subject.

"Nope. In fact, ain't none of them taken a break and come down."

"Well," Clint said, "I better go up and have a look."

"Your man Jensen's up there."

"Thanks."

Clint took the beer with him upstairs. As he entered, Billy Jensen was taking a walk around the table. He broke off and approached Clint.

"How's it going?"

"Short's winnin', but the others are stickin' around," Jensen said.

"Take a break."

"I just relieved Walt about an hour ago."

"That's okay," Clint said. "Take a break anyway. Get a beer and then come back."

"Suits me."

Jensen left. Clint carried his beer across the room, took up position where Short could see him. When he did, the little gambler excused himself from the table and walked over. "Been trying to get a chance to talk to you," he said.

"What about?"

"Miles," Short said. "He had a talk with that other feller again, didn't try to make like they didn't know each other, this time. But he said he was askin' directions. If he was askin' directions, wouldn't he ask the bartender? Who would know better?"

"Wait a minute. Directions?"

"That's what he said."

"There was just a guy downstairs, left a message for Miles with the bartender. Something about directions."

"Tall fella, black hat? Vest? Wears his gun down low?" Short asked.

"Could be. I just saw him leaving the saloon, didn't get a real good look. But that sounds like him."

"And there's another thing."

"What?"

"Miles and this other fella McCloud? They ain't playin' to win."

"What are they playing for?"

"To last. Jack and me are playin' to win."

"Okay," Clint said. "Thanks, Luke. You better get back now."

"Okay." Short stated back, then stopped and turned. "You need anythin', you let me know."

"I will."

Clint watched the game, nursed his beer, and waited for Jensen to get back. When he did, Clint went back down to talk to the bartender.

"Another?"

"Nope," Clint said. "I need you to tell me about that message that fella left for Vince Miles."

"I ain't supposed to—"

"I know," Clint said, "but I won't tell anybody you told me. It's important."

"Well, okay," the bartender said. "Can't see no harm. He said to tell that Miles fella that the directions he gave him won't be good until tomorrow."

"That's it?"

"That's it. You know what that means?"

"Don't have a clue," Clint said, but he did. He thought he had a big clue.

FORTY-TWO

The only person Clint thought he could confide in was Luke Short. So he waited until the next morning, figuring he'd find Short having breakfast at Chuck's.

He was right.

He had gone to his own room to turn in the night before without stopping at Brenda's room first. He knew what she said, but her fight against the Mauler had been tougher than she had anticipated. He decided to let her have a whole night's sleep in order to recuperate. After all, she did have another fight coming up.

When he walked into Chuck's, the waitress asked, "Joinin' your friend again?"

"Yes, I am."

"Well, go ahead, then. Steak and eggs?"

"Of course."

"I'll bring you some coffee."

Clint walked over to Short's table, sat opposite his friend.

"'Mornin'," Short said. "You figure the mystery out yet?"

"I think something's going to happen today," Clint said. "The mystery is, what?"

"And that's the part you ain't figured out yet," Short said.

"Right."

"Well, what are you gonna do about it?"

"I think I'm going to eat breakfast, talk it over with you," Clint said, "and you and me are going to figure it out . . ."

"It has to have something to do with the government," Clint said.

"What makes you say that?"

Clint couldn't tell him the truth, so he said, "Let's call it a hunch."

Short gave Clint a funny look. Hunches usually have some basis in fact, and he wasn't aware of any facts that would lead Clint to this hunch.

"If you say so."

"I think what we'll have to do is keep an eye on Vince Miles," Clint said, "and find the man he was talking to."

"Well, I can keep an eye on him, since he'll be sitting at the table with me. The game starts early today."

"Luke, I wasn't going to ask you—"

"You didn't ask," Short said. "I offered."

"Okay, thanks," Clint said. "I'll have to find the other man. I'll check with the bartender again. Maybe he heard a name."

"So we'll walk back to the Colorado together," Short said.

"Fine."

They paid their bill and headed for the saloon.

* * *

When they got to the saloon, the doors were open to allow the players entry, but there were no other customers.

Seated at a back table, drinking coffee, was Mike McCloud.

"What do you know about him?" Clint asked Short.

"Nothin', except that he's not playin' to win, like I told you."

"I think I'll talk to him while I have the chance," Clint said.

"I'll go upstairs, see if Miles is there yet."

"Okay," Clint said. "See you later."

Clint stopped at the bar first to ask the bartender about the man who had come to see Miles.

"Nope," the man said, "I never heard no name for the guy."

"Okay," Clint said. "How's that fellow taking his coffee?"

"Black."

"Give me two cups of black."

Armed with coffee, Clint walked to Mike McCloud's table.

"Fresh cup?" Clint asked, sitting and sliding one across the table.

"Thanks," McCloud said. "Was wondering when we'd get a chance to talk. Figured if I sat here long enough . . ."

"Good to see you . . . Mike."

"You too, Clint."

"Now, why are you here pretending to be a poker player?" Clint asked.

"We got wind that something was up in this area," McCloud said.

"That's it? You got wind?"

McCloud shrugged; Clint figured that was all he was going to get from the man.

"Okay, so when and where?" Clint asked.

"That's why I'm here," McCloud said. "To find that out."

"Well," Clint said, "I might be able to help there . . ."

McCloud listened intently while Clint told him about his hunch.

"And you made that leap based on the fact that I'm here?"

"Well, yeah."

"I can see where that would confuse Short."

"I couldn't tell him about you," Clint said. "I know better than that."

"Thanks. Okay, so Vince Miles has got something going with this other fella, who you're going to try and find."

"Right."

"And Short's going to keep an eye on Miles."

"Right again."

Mike McCloud gave the situation some thought, then said, "I think it might be time for me to bust out of this game."

FORTY-THREE

Clint tried to conjure up the image of the man who had been leaving the Colorado as he got there the previous day. Tall, black hat, a confident walk, but none of that would make him stand out.

If something was being planned—as McCloud had indicated—then the festival was to be used as a diversion. He doubted that Joe Nicholas had invested so much of his time and money in something that was meant as a diversion. That left the mayor. He must have known that this festival had little chance of succeeding, but the politician must have figured it would make a good cover for other activities.

So whatever was happening, the mayor was part of it. Maybe even the brains behind it. He'd have to know all of the others who were involved—Vince Miles, the man Clint was looking for, and who knew how many others? There had to be guns for hire involved—maybe even Clint's two bushwhackers?

Clint had been heading for the river but he changed direction now and headed for City Hall.

* * *

When Clint got to the mayor's door, he did just what Sheriff Abernathy did. He barged in without knocking.

"Damn it, Abernathy—" the mayor started, but he stopped when he saw that Clint was not the sheriff.

"Hello, Mr. Mayor."

"Oh, uh, Mr. Adams. I, uh, am pretty busy here—" the man stammered.

"I won't bother you for long, Mayor," Clint said. "I just want to give you a chance to reconsider your answer to my previous question."

"W-what question was that?"

"I'll simplify it for you," Clint said. "What the hell is going on?"

"I don't—"

"Don't tell me you don't know what's going on," Clint said, cutting the man off. "This festival is being used as a diversion. You're going to tell me what the diversion is for."

"Mr. Adams," the man said, trying not to let his voice squeak, "I'm the mayor—"

"You've got two choices," Clint said. "I can put a bullet in your leg, or throw you out the window. The fall might break more than just a leg, so I'd probably take the bullet—"

"It wasn't my idea!" Mayor Soames shouted, holding his chubby hands up in front of his face.

"Put your hands down," Clint said, "and start at the beginning."

Rusty Cooper watched as Clint left the City Hall building and walked off purposefully. Given the direction he was going, Cooper figured he was going down to the river, probably to talk with Joe Nicholas.

He had spotted Clint going in, found a spot across the

street to watch from. If Clint Adams was going to talk to the mayor alone, it was bad news.

Cooper waited until Clint was out of sight, then crossed the street and entered the building.

Clint left the mayor's office with a name: Rusty Cooper. He knew it. Cooper was for hire, but Clint had never met him. He was sure he had seen him, though, coming out of the saloon.

There were two men who might help him find Cooper. Vince Miles was one of them. The other was Joe Nicholas. Nicholas had been uncomfortable about his festival from the moment Clint arrived in town, and Clint had seen him coming out of City Hall.

He knew Miles was at the poker game, and he could find him there anytime, so he headed for the river to see if he could find Nicky.

So far the members of this "gang" were the mayor, Rusty Cooper, and Vince Miles. There had to be hired guns in there, somewhere. What Clint needed to find out was how many.

FORTY-FOUR

There were wrestling matches going on, but there weren't many spectators. Joe Nicholas was there, looking miserable. Clint thought he was about to add to his misery.

"Rusty Cooper," he said, as he came up next to him.

"What?" Nicholas turned and stared at him, wide-eyed.

"Where can I find him, Joe?"

Nicholas frowned, then looked back into the ring where two men with big bellies were grappling.

"Don't play dumb with me, Nicky," Clint said. "I talked to the mayor."

"What?" The wide-eyed look again.

"He told me everything."

"Everything?"

"All that he knows," Clint said. "Now I need to know what you know."

"Me? Nothin'!" Nicholas said. "The mayor told me I could have the festival here if . . ."

"If what?"

"If I got you here."

"Me? What for?"

"I don't know," Nicholas said. "He didn't tell you that, huh?"

"No, he didn't," Clint said. "But I'm going to ask him."

Clint barged into the mayor's office again.

"Damn it, Soames, this time—" he started, but he stopped when he saw the man sitting in his chair. He knew a dead man when he saw one.

He moved to the desk, saw the bloody wound in the mayor's stomach. Someone had come in here right after he'd left and killed him. That someone had to be Rusty Cooper.

His next move was still the same.

Find Cooper.

Cooper found Fields and Barnes in Saloon #8.

"Time to go," he said.

"What, now?" Fields asked.

"Yes, now."

"I thought it wasn't until tomorrow."

"It is," Cooper said, "but we have to leave now. Adams is lookin' for us."

The two men jumped to their feet.

"He is?" Fields asked.

"How does he know about us?" Barnes asked.

"The mayor talked," Cooper said.

"About everythin'?" Fields asked.

"We don't even know about everythin'," Barnes said.

"Come with me," Cooper said, "and I'll tell you on the way."

They left Saloon #8. Out front, Cooper said, "Go get your horses and meet me back here."

"Where are you goin'?" Fields asked.

"I've got to do one more thing."

"What?"

"Just go!"

The Gunsmith considered his options: Report the shooting to the sheriff or let someone else find the body? If he reported it, the sheriff would have questions—lots of questions. There was no time. He needed to find Cooper, and whoever he was using to do his grunt work.

He needed help, so he headed for the Colorado.

Cooper entered the Colorado, approached the bar. The place was half full, but the patrons ignored him and he ignored them.

"Back for more directions?" the barman asked.

"I want to go upstairs," Cooper said.

"Sorry, can't—"

"Take me up," Cooper said, "or I'll kill you."

"What?"

"Don't even think about going for the shotgun under the bar," Cooper said. "You'll be dead before I touch it."

"What?" the bartender said again.

"Keep your hands where I can see them," Cooper said, "And walk me upstairs. Now!"

When Clint got to the Colorado Saloon, there was nobody behind the bar. There were a few men standing at the bar, others seated around the room, and a couple of girls working the floor.

No bartender.

One of the girls came to the bar with her tray.

"Where's the bartender?" Clint asked her.

"That's what I want to know."

"Aren't there usually two?" He recalled having seen two the first time he came in, but not since.

"Only when we're real busy," she said. "Haven't been real busy in a while."

"So where did this one go?"

"I told you, I don't know. And I need some drinks."

Clint turned to the men at the bar.

"Where'd the bartender go?"

Three of them just stared at him, but the fourth said, "He went through that curtain with another man."

"When?"

"Ten minutes ago."

He turned and looked at the girl. "Better get your own drinks." He went through the curtain.

When Clint got upstairs, he took out his gun and moved down the hall as quickly and quietly as he could. When he burst into the poker room, he was surprised at what he saw.

FORTY-FIVE

Clint untied Luke Short and Mike McCloud. Three-Fingered Jack wasn't tied, because he was dead. Somebody had stabbed him. The girl who was the dealer was also gagged and tied.

"He surprised us by sending the bartender in first," Short said. "Got the drop on us after that."

"What about Jack?"

"He was mad because he'd just started winning," Short said. "Cooper got him with his knife. Threw it. He's good."

Clint noticed Short was favoring his right hand.

"What happened to you?"

"He smashed my hand with his gun," Short said.

"Why didn't he just kill all of you?" Clint asked.

"It would've been too noisy with his gun, and taken too long with his knife. So he tied us up and left, with Miles. What are they up to?"

"They're going to pull a robbery."

"What are they stealin'?"

"I don't know," Clint said, "but they're going to steal it from the U.S. Government."

Clint untied McCloud, but he wasn't moving.

"Damnit, come on," Clint said, slapping his face.

Nothing.

He felt the pulse in his neck. It was strong, but the man was out. A blow to the head will do that.

"Okay," Clint said. "We need to get him to a doctor. Untie the girl. We'll send her."

"What about the sheriff?"

"Yeah," Clint said, "we're going to need him, too. I have something else to tell him, too."

"What?"

"You'll find out," he said. "Let's get McCloud taken care of."

As Clint had suspected it would, it took hours to explain everything to the sheriff's satisfaction. Short was waiting outside the sheriff's office when Clint came out.

"What now?" Short asked.

"I've got to find out where this job is taking place," Clint said. "Then I have to get there and stop it."

"Alone?"

"You can't come," Clint said. "Not with that hand."

Short looked down at his bandaged hand.

"And McCloud's in no shape," Clint said. "He's still dizzy."

"There's got to be somebody who can go with you," Short said.

"Actually," Clint said, "there might be. Come on."

"Let me get this straight," David Flanagan said. "You want me to help you stop a robbery?"

"That's right," Clint said.

"Why should I do that?"

"You'd be doing a service for the United States Government."

Flanagan looked at Julie, who grinned at him.

"You want me to risk my life for that?" Flanagan asked.

"Hey, you're Wild Bill Flanagan."

"I told you I've never fired a shot at a man before," Flanagan said. "I may have to kill somebody if I help you. You've got to give me something to make it worth that."

Clint stared at Flanagan. He knew there was only one thing Wild Bill Flanagan wanted, and he also knew he had to give it to him.

FORTY-SIX

Five miles outside of town, Rusty Cooper sat atop a rise with both Fields and Barnes, staring down at a road below them.

"You sure it's comin'?" Fields asked.

"It's supposed to be comin' on that road," Cooper said.

"When?" Barnes asked.

"This mornin'."

"We gonna sit up here all mornin'?" Fields asked.

Cooper looked at him.

"We're gonna sit up here as long as it takes."

"Good thing for you it's not going to take that long," a voice said from behind them.

Cooper turned in his saddle and saw Clint Adams. Two men were with him: Luke Short, who had a shotgun in the crook of his arm, and another man who wore buckskins and two six-guns.

"What the hell are you doin' here?" Cooper asked.

"I'm here to stop you and your men, Cooper," Clint said.

"You know," Cooper said, "I was gonna take care of you

later, Adams. But I can do it just as well now. And my
friend, here, will take care of your crippled friend, and your
friend in the costume."

Fields and Barnes exchanged a doubtful look. They hadn't
signed on for this.

Cooper looked down at the road. Nothing yet.

He dismounted. "I tell you what, Adams," he said. "Just
you and me."

He handed his reins to Fields and said to both men,
"When he draws, kill him."

"But what about—" Fields said.

"I'll take the other two," he said. "You two wanted to
kill Adams, right? Well, here's your chance, while he's con-
centratin' on me."

The two men exchanged a glance, nodding to each other.

"This could work," Fields said.

Cooper nodded, then turned to face Clint. Flanagan and
Short had cleared out, giving Clint room.

"Anytime, Cooper," Clint said.

This would work, Cooper thought. All he had to do was
kill Short and the other man.

He drew.

Clint suspected Cooper would try something, so he'd warned
Flanagan to watch the other two men.

Now, as Cooper drew, Flanagan saw the other men going for their guns. They were slow—painfully slow. He knew
he didn't have to kill them. He fired twice, once with each
hand, and their guns went spinning away.

Luke Short didn't even have time to shift his shotgun,
Flanagan had fired that quickly.

He was impressed.

*　　*　　*

Clint drew his gun and fired before Cooper could clear leather. The bullet hit Cooper in the center of the chest. There was a momentary look of shock on his face before his expression went blank and he fell on his back.

Clint walked to the body, kicked the gun away just to be sure. Then he looked at the two mounted men. Both were holding their injured hands.

"H-hey," Fields said, "we got no guns."

"Drop your rifles to the ground."

They obeyed, each using their left hands.

"Now ride. If I see you again, I'll kill you both."

They both grabbed their horses' reins, turned, and rode off at a gallop.

"Hey, Clint," Short called.

Clint walked over to where his friend was standing, Flanagan came over, as well. They all looked down at the road below them, where a single wagon was traveling. There was one driver, no guards. It looked like a prison wagon, but Clint figured there was something other than prisoners inside. Something valuable, and important.

"That can't be the wagon," Short said.

"I don't see another one."

"How did you find out where they'd be?"

"McCloud told me."

"How did he know?" Flanagan asked.

Clint couldn't tell them that McCloud's real name was Jim West, and that he was a government agent. There were things West wouldn't tell him, and things he couldn't tell Flanagan and Short. But West had known what road the wagon was taking, and Clint had been able to pick out the best place to observe and take it from.

"A little birdie must have told him."

"But what's in the wagon?" Flanagan asked.

"I don't know," Clint said. "But it's not important."

"Aren't you even curious?"

"No."

They watched as the wagon passed by safely, and continued on.

"And you," Clint said to Flanagan.

"What?"

"Save the fancy shooting for the stage," Clint said. "If and when you ever have to draw on another man again, shoot to kill."

"But I shot their guns—"

"This time," Clint said.

FORTY-SEVEN

That night, Brenda had her last fight and won easily, knocking the man out in two rounds. Her opponent never touched her. She was bathed and freshly dressed by the time Clint and Wild Bill Flanagan were set up for their shooting exhibition. Clint had set it up so that they'd be shooting together, not against each other. Flanagan accepted that offer, and then agreed to help Clint.

"I don't understand why the mayor and Cooper wanted me to invite Clint to the festival," Nicholas said to Short. They were both right in front of the stage so they wouldn't miss a thing. Brenda was standing with them. By the time Clint, Short, and Flanagan had returned to town, Jim West had gone, even though the doctor had told him not to ride for a while.

"Cooper wanted to take Clint," Short said. "That would have been an even bigger distraction from what they were planning to do."

"He was foolish enough to think he could do that?" Nicholas asked.

"He was arrogant enough to think he'd figure out a way," Short said. "Arrogance gets more men killed, Joe. Remember that."

"Speaking of arrogance, the whole thing was the mayor's idea?"

"He got the word from some political contact in Washington that the wagon would be passing near his town," Short said. "Then he got in touch with Cooper, and they planned it."

"But not well enough, huh?" Nicholas said.

"No," Short said, "not nearly well enough. By the way, Clint's not very happy with you."

"Me. What'd I do?"

"Whatever," Short said. "I'd just stay away from him if I was you."

"Tell me again why Clint wouldn't shoot against Flanagan?" Brenda asked Short.

"Shootin' against Clint and losin' would do nothin' for the kid," Short said.

"And Clint was that sure he'd beat him?"

Short smiled.

"Believe me," he said, "he would beat him, every time. This way, it may help Flanagan's reputation to be able to say he shot with the Gunsmith."

"Well," she said, as Clint and Flanagan got set to shoot at a series of stationary and moving targets, "this should be interesting."

"Personally," Luke Short said, flexing the fingers of his right hand, "I've had enough of interestin' for a while."

Watch for

THE TRIAL OF BAT MASTERSON

351st novel in the exciting GUNSMITH series
from Jove

Coming in March!

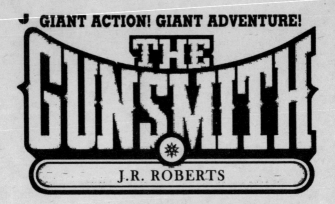

GIANT ACTION! GIANT ADVENTURE!

THE GUNSMITH

J.R. ROBERTS

penguin.com/actionwesterns

M455AS0510

ISBN 978-0-515-14900-5

14900

THE MA

When an old friend ropes Clint Adams into providing security for the Colorado River Festival, he finds himself in the one-horse town of Bullhead City. Keeping an eye out for potential thieves and troublemakers at the sporting exhibitions, Clint befriends female boxer Brenda "The Bomb" Mitchell—who's just as good between the sheets as she is between the ropes.

But when "Wild Bill" Flanagan challenges the famous Gunsmith to a shooting contest, Clint realizes he's been duped into the role of the festival's star attraction—though he's really just being used as a diversion from some sinister doings...

OVER FIVE MILLION GUNSMITH BOOKS IN PRINT!

To find out more about your favorite Westerns, visit www.penguin.com/actionwesterns

www.penguin.com

ISBN 978-0-515-14900-5

50599

9 780515 149005

$5.99 U.S.
$7.50 CAN